SUPERB WRITING
TO FIRE THE IMAGINATION

Judy Allen says, 'The place where a story is set may not always be the first thing I think about, but once I've chosen it (or it's chosen me) it becomes as important as any of the events, ideas or characters – in fact it is one of the characters. Places with powerful spirits have always spoken to the human imagination, and for thousands of years people have responded to them, perhaps planting sacred groves, building shrines, setting up standing stones – or creating stories. I find myself wondering whether there are forces we know nothing about but which are as powerful and relentless as gravity or the struggle for life.'

Her *AWAITING DEVELOPMENTS* won the Whitbread Award and the Friends of the Earth Earthworm Award. Author of more than 50 books including *THE BURNING, THE SPRING ON THE MOUNTAIN, THE DREAM THING* and *BETWEEN THE MOON AND THE ROCK*, she also writes for radio.

THE STONES OF THE MOON

JUDY ALLEN

**Hodder
Children's
Books**

a division of Hodder Headline

To T. J.

First published in Great Britain in 1975
by Jonathan Cape Ltd

This edition published by Hodder Children's Books in 2000

10 9 8 7 6 5 4 3 2 1

A Catalogue record for this book is available from
the British Library

ISBN 0 340 74024 8

Typeset by Avon Dataset Ltd, Bidford-on-Avon, Warks

Printed and bound in Great Britain by
The Guernsey Press Co. Ltd, Channel Isles

Hodder Children's Books
A Division of Hodder Headline
338 Euston Road
London NW1 3BH

ONE

The Ordnance Survey map was beginning to crumple slightly in the damp, and David folded it up, not without some difficulty, and put it in the pocket of his waterproof jacket. He didn't need to look at it again, in any case, until he had crossed the stone bridge.

His jacket, which was new and bright yellow, had an attached hood, but he didn't put it up. Although this year was going on record for the coolest and wettest July in the last twenty, it wasn't actually raining. It was just that the air was full of a clinging dampness that drifted down from the moors and spread over the grey town like a sea mist. Anyway, the jacket embarrassed him enough with its newness and brightness. He felt the pixie-hood appendage was best ignored.

A Sunday morning quietness was on the town and he met no one. He passed the last house and walked down the narrow road towards the river. It was quite deep and free-flowing at this point and he couldn't hear it.

The road was unhedged and to his left he could look across an area of wasteland, too damp for building, where a few sheep strayed. And to his right a double line of stakes straddled roughly-cleared ground, scarred with the spoor of earth-moving machines, indicating the line of the new motorway.

The road he was walking crossed an old stone bridge. It was a beautiful bridge but it was not wide enough to bear the volume of traffic that would be taking a short cut across this corner of Yorkshire as soon as the new motorway link-up was completed. And when it had been completed, this town would be for ever doomed to be on the way to somewhere else, never more a place in its own right. He wondered if anyone minded.

The motorway bridge wasn't built yet, but work on the approaches was well under way. He stood leaning on the parapet, looking up-river at the immense earthworks on both sides. Especially he looked at the works on the town side of the river, where they had made the discovery and where, presumably, his father was pottering right now, although the volunteers wouldn't arrive until tomorrow. He could see no sign of movement. Whatever was going on down there must be happening behind the great mound of earth and rubble that rose steeply, almost like a dam wall, on this side of the excavation.

No car passed. Nothing moved.

David took out the map again, folded it down to the relevant square, and looked around. From the other side of the river the ground sloped upwards to a featureless horizon. Somewhere up there was the stone circle he was looking for. The road, having crossed the bridge, set off in both directions. Down to the right it merged into the mess that was going to be the motorway. To the left it passed a large, bleak, factory-like building with high chimneys before it disappeared from view.

He put his finger on the map. 'You are here,' he said

aloud. A movement caught his eye and he crossed to the other parapet. Between the bridge and the factory-like building a boy and girl were crouched at the water's edge. Three jam-jars full of water and a home-made net were beside them, but they appeared just now to be observing rather than fishing and very absorbed in whatever they could see. David wondered if they had heard him say 'You are here', but they were quite a little way away and far too intent on whatever they were doing to look up. The boy seemed to be about his own age, and too old to fish with jam-jars, David thought. The girl didn't look much younger. He withdrew quickly to the other parapet, taking his shiny yellowness out of their range of vision. He returned to the map, running his finger along the brown contour lines. They seemed to suggest that the ridge in front of him went on rising well beyond what looked, from the bridge, to be the top.

The best landmark lay between the factory and the bridge. A deep natural cleft cut right back into the slope, almost to the summit. It seemed to him that if he climbed the bank parallel to the cleft and continued walking he should reach his objective. He put the map away again, crossed the bridge and the road, and began to walk up a slope that was steeper and wetter than he had expected. He went as quickly as he could, trying to take the ground by surprise and sometimes using his hands. He was very conscious that he was now in full view of the boy and girl at the river's edge, should they chance to glance round, and he kept up maximum speed until he reached a narrow plateau, the skyline he had seen from the bridge.

From here the ground rose gradually to a new skyline – featureless ground with short, coarse grass and patches of bracken, heather and agonizing gorse.

He stood looking round at the view, not minding so much if he was seen now that he was no longer crawling about like an ungainly yellow spider.

From here he could see his father down on the site, moving jerkily about like a little ant while another figure, presumably the president of the local archaeological society, stood by and watched him. 'Come with me,' his father had said, but the Romans had never appealed to David. The thought that his father was about to preside over the uncovering of one of their mosaics held no magic for him.

He stood still, looking down, aware that he was deliberately postponing the moment of actually finding the circle – like leaving the marzipan on the cake until last.

He couldn't have explained why he wanted to find it. Only twice before had he seen stone circles, both in the Scottish border country where his father had been supervising the excavation of a Roman villa, interesting for its relatively far northern position.

The first one had been a fine circle, almost complete; the grey weathered stones, pitted like chewed nougat, standing as tall as his father. It was David's first experience of anything so ancient and he had stayed with it until his father insisted they move on – walking among the stones, touching them, asking questions to which it seemed there were no answers. The tiny local museum had had little to

4

say about it. The centre had once been excavated but all that had been found were the remains of a cremation, thousands of years old. No one was even certain that the cremators and the circle builders were the same people. The stones and their relationships to each other had been measured but the measurements were lost and any conclusions long since forgotten.

He had heard about the second circle from the curator of the museum, who was anxious to help and distressed that he could offer so little information. The curator had described its location, and David's father, in a benevolent mood at the successful culmination of his Roman investigations, had helped him to find it where it clung just below the crest of a bleak ridge, a couple of miles from the nearest track. That circle had been small, ground down by wind and weather, the top of the tallest stone no more than a hand's breadth above ground. The circle was incomplete, with two or three stones flung some distance away, embedded deeply in the earth, as though the ground had moved or vandals had attacked the structure centuries before. Old records showed that the area had a history of floods, and David's father had suggested that these might be responsible for the destruction. But to David these small, worn stones, crouched low in rough, dark grass and visited only by ravens and straying sheep, had no less power than the first tall circle they had seen from the road. 'Why?' he kept saying. 'What were they for?' But his father was drawn to Roman archaeology and said that it was a waste of energy to beat your brains out over something so lost

5

in antiquity that no useful clues remained.

And now summer work had begun on the site in Yorkshire and David, dutifully examining the Ordnance Survey map to see where they would live for the duration, had noticed the now familiar little ring of dots. Under them, in archaic writing, were the words Weeping Stones. That, for him, charged the entire summer project with an excitement as great as his father's.

This time he would have weeks in which to explore, instead of discovering something on the last day and having to go home, leaving it to continue its slow disintegration, not even partly understood.

He moved across to the cleft which, according to the map, pointed to the circle like a crooked finger. It was almost too narrow to fall down at this point, but very, very deep. He walked along its edge, lay on his stomach and peered into it. The sides were practically sheer and covered with ferns. As it widened out towards the river it became shallower and shrubs grew at the bottom. He could look right along it to its widest point. Beyond, he could see part of the road, and over the road the factory-like building and, near to it, on the mud and shingle beaches of the river's edge, the crouched figures of the boy and girl, tiny in the distance.

He got to his feet and set off upwards and to the right, heading in the direction indicated by the cleft. He had taken perhaps twenty steps when the stone circle seemed to rise out of the coarse grass on the skyline in front of him.

It seemed to David that it was complete, not because

it was a precise circle – it wasn't, it looked more like an ellipse – but because the stones seemed to be equally spaced one from another.

He moved closer.

They were quite large, these stones. The two tallest would reach, he could see, to his shoulder or higher. The smallest had been worn down to knee height, or perhaps they had been sucked down into the ground. Perhaps each stone was several metres high and in the secret world under the earth stood an immense structure, its very top breaking the surface of the ground, as rocks break the surface of the sea. And like surf the stubby grass broke against the pitted stones.

The Weeping Stones, standing, leaning, alone on a moorland ridge, worn down by their journey through time, carrying nothing with them to indicate their purpose; unless, perhaps, their purpose was plain enough to anyone perceptive enough to interpret it.

The stones leaned, this way and that, leaned together as if they were whispering, and a light breeze moved the grass against their roots and drew a thread of mist over their heads and away.

David's heart was beating so hard that the circle seemed to his eyes to move in rhythm. He waited until his initial excitement had died down before moving in. He wanted to touch, to examine, to explore, to pace out the distance between the stones, to look up at the sky and down at the earth as he had done before, trying to understand.

He moved into the circle, at the edge. He stood –

forming a part of it himself and looking across its width – and suddenly he felt uncomfortable.

A sensation, not quite of dread but certainly of unease, had dropped upon him. He had no idea why. Down below he could still see half the town, though the river and the earthworks were cut off from him by the ridge he had climbed. The town looked remote and still. It had no reality. Only he had reality – he who was alive and the stones which were not. Or at any rate were not the same form of life as he was – because in their way they *were* alive.

He was standing between the two tallest stones. They leaned towards him, not touching him, two tall, hard, grey shapes, heavy matter, damp with the mist. It was as if they were in communion with each other – something was passing between them and he had broken the circuit. He stepped forward into the circle, and the uncomfortable feeling left him to be replaced by a growing fear. He had broken into something, disturbed a pattern. Now he was out of the way and the chain of communication was resumed. He was alone in the centre, the marshy centre where the trefoil grew, flesh and blood in a community of stone, an alien community which was somehow conscious in a way he did not understand.

He didn't feel threatened, only afraid. He didn't believe that they wished him harm, only that they were dangerous, unimaginably dangerous, just as heavy machinery in action is dangerous.

He ran out from the circle, out from between the two tallest stones, and his heel skidded on the marshy ground and his hand, flung out involuntarily to save himself, touched the stone on the right. An electric shock cracked up his right arm and into his shoulder and he fell, and rolled, and lay, discarded from the ellipse of stones on to the damp ground beyond.

TWO

David got down to the level of the road again and hesitated before the bridge. He had found the circle, and just for the moment there seemed to be nowhere to go. He rubbed his arm. It felt all right. Already he was beginning to think he had imagined the shock. Certainly his arm had forgotten it as if it had never happened, although his hip and leg felt bruised where he had fallen.

He stretched out his hand and stroked the edge of the bridge – cool, damp, old stone. The bridge was very old, and beautiful in its simplicity, but such a new thing, such a domestic thing, compared with the circle. And yet – as far as he could tell – made from the same stone.

Still he stood, and considered his next move, trying not to face the idea that the freedom of the next two months might after all be a burden. He ran through the possibilities in his mind. He could climb back up the slope and re-examine the standing stones. There was no one to hurry him along as before, he had plenty of time. He could join his father on the site. Or he could walk along the river's edge, check what wild life it seemed to support, try to guess what those two might be fishing for. From this distance the water looked pure and clean, although he had a townsman's distrust of the building with the tall chimneys.

He considered all these alternatives but, slightly to his own surprise, he pursued none of them. Deliberately he slithered down the slope beside the bridge and crunched over shingle towards the two figures who still worked from the river bank. He stood there, looming over them, until they were forced to look round.

'Hallo,' said the boy, after a pause. 'On holiday, are you?' He began to write something on a damp piece of paper which lay on the ground beside him. He didn't seem to be planning on listening to David's answer.

'We may be here for about two months,' said David. 'My father's an archaeologist – he's in charge of the excavations at the motorway site.' He'd had a variety of responses to that kind of statement in the past, but this was the first time he had no response at all. The boy's pencil worked its slow way across the soggy paper and the girl tipped her head so that she could see what he was writing.

'When the workmen began digging to build the motorway bridge, they found part of a Roman mosaic,' said David. 'My father is supposed to be an expert on Roman archaeology – that's why he's here.' He paused. 'If it looks good, they may shift the whole thing to York Museum.'

The other boy glanced down-river and continued to make notes.

'And right now,' said David, 'thirty-four purple elephants wearing green hats are crossing the bridge behind you.'

The boy put the pencil into his inside jacket pocket,

then folded the paper and slipped it into the same pocket. 'Let's hope the elephants don't damage the mosaic,' he said.

'Oh,' said David. 'I thought you weren't listening.'

'Are you going to work on the site?'

'No – I'm not interested in Roman stuff. I'm interested in the stone circle up there.'

All at once he had the girl's full attention, and the boy laughed. 'You're as bad as Jane,' he said. 'She's always up there.'

David brightened and moved closer. 'Can you tell me anything about it?' he said.

He spoke directly to Jane, but she just sat back on her heels and stared. Her face seemed alive and intelligent but she looked at him as if he was speaking in a foreign language.

'It's up there,' said the boy, waving his arm vaguely and not looking where he pointed.

'I've been to it,' said David. 'I've just come down. But I thought – if you're interested in it – you might know something about it.'

The river sighed on past them and the shingle creaked a little under David's feet.

'It's called the Weeping Stones,' said the boy. 'That's all anybody knows. And she's called Jane and I'm called Tim, so what are you called?'

David told him, moved in closer, and crouched down so that he was on a level with them.

'What do *you* know about it?' he said across Tim to Jane. 'Only – I felt very strange up there . . .'

Her face was half hidden by a curtain of long, damp hair. He wanted to shake her to bring some response from her. It even occurred to him to wonder if she had a speech impediment. He stared at her unwaveringly and she shifted her position slightly.

'It often is strange up there,' she said at last, very quietly. 'Sometimes the circle shuts you out.'

'Yes, that's exactly it, exactly it,' said David.

Tim put on an exaggerated Yorkshire accent. 'Aye, lad, none of us locals 'll go up there on us own.'

'Honestly?' said David.

'Of course not "honestly". I made it up.'

David ignored him and returned to Jane. 'The really weird thing,' he said, 'is that I touched one of the stones and I thought I got a shock – like an electric shock.'

It was as if she didn't want to respond to what he was saying but couldn't help it. She even gave him half a smile. 'One of the two tall ones,' she said.

'Yes!'

She nodded. 'I've felt it.'

'Rubbish,' said Tim, suddenly no longer preoccupied with jam-jars and notes.

'*Not* rubbish.'

'You've never told me about it.'

'I knew you'd say "rubbish". But he felt it, too.'

Tim looked to David. 'You're sure?'

'Well I wasn't quite sure a minute ago. I slipped and put out my hand and sort of hit the stone. I wasn't quite sure if I just jarred my arm or if I really did get a shock. At least, I was sure at the time that it was a shock but I began to doubt it on the way down. But if someone else has felt it . . .'

He was very aware that in his attempt to be totally honest he had lost all conviction. He should simply have said, 'Yes. I am sure.' But then – he wasn't.

'Imagination,' said Tim, firmly but not unkindly. 'And she's got plenty of that.'

'I promise you,' said Jane. 'It wasn't strong, but I felt it.'

'How often?' said David.

'Once.'

'When?'

'Oh . . . about a year ago.' Her voice, already almost inaudible, dropped still lower. 'It was on my birthday,' she said. 'I always go up there on my birthday.'

'And you never said – all this time?' said Tim.

'I was waiting to see if it would happen again. And I didn't think you'd believe me.'

'I don't.'

She scowled at him.

'You were mistaken, is all I mean. How could you possibly get an electric shock from an old stone? If you knew anything about electricity you'd see what I mean.'

'Nobody knows anything about electricity,' said Jane.

'But do you know anything about the circle?' said David. 'Do you know if it's ever been excavated? I mean, *is* anything known about it?'

Jane shook her head.

'She goes up there and moons about from time to time,' said Tim. 'She doesn't know any more about it than anyone else.'

'Well I mean to find out everything about it,' said David, getting up because his foot was going to sleep.

'You can't,' said Jane, almost fiercely. 'It's a secret.'

'Your secret?' said David.

'Of course not.'

'Whose then?'

'Nobody's. It's its own secret. Nobody will ever know – it won't let them.' She glared at David. 'But I can go there any time,' she added.

'Anybody can,' said David. 'It's not difficult to reach.'

Jane picked up two of the jam-jars, apparently at random, by their string loops. 'I'm going home,' she said. And did.

Tim got on with what he was doing, scraping about in the sludge at the river's edge. 'She's got toothache,' he said.

'What a shame,' said David automatically. 'Do you go fishing?'

'No. Why?'

'I thought you might be digging for worms.'

'If you want to know what I'm doing, why don't you just ask?'

David felt the colour rising to his face, but Tim was still bent over the water.

'What *are* you doing, then?'

'Pollution survey.'

'Oh really? Oh, that's interesting. I'm very interested in pollution.'

Tim glanced round at him and away again. He had slopped some mud into the plastic dish and was collecting his belongings together. Cloudy water swirled in the jar and waterweed clung to the net.

'Was it your own idea?' David persisted. He knew that his questions were buzzing around Tim's head like wasps, and that the more he asked the less response he would get, but he couldn't seem to help himself. It was partly that he actually wanted answers – but more that his own need to break through the barrier grew as Tim strengthened his defences.

'School project.'

'Are you checking up on that factory?'

'It's a textile mill.'

Tim stood up, the remaining jar hanging from his wrist, the dish in one hand and the net in the other.

'How do you do the survey, then?'

'Take samples from the river, above and below the mill. Compare the results.'

The two faced each other.

'Could I help?' said David. And then, quickly, in case he was turned down, 'Except that I'll be a bit busy, finding out about those stones.'

'We'll be down again after school tomorrow,' said Tim. 'Below the mill.'

THREE

Unsure if he had made friends or not, and with a strange sense of loss now that he had found the circle, David followed Tim over the bridge and then turned left across the rutted ground towards the site. He glanced round once or twice to see Tim making his way steadily along the road to the town, but Tim didn't look back.

As he got nearer to the site, David could see that his father had been left on his own and that he was even now engaged with what was presumably the first of many casual inquirers; a tall man in jeans and patched sweater, with greying hair that drifted around his shoulders.

David made his way towards them.

His father was dealing with the inquiry with the mixture of impatience and politeness he always employed on such occasions.

'We hope to start tomorrow,' he was saying. 'But we already have sufficient volunteer workers.'

'I wasn't volunteering. Just taking an interest.' The man turned and smiled as David joined them a little hesitantly, not sure whether their conversation was ending or beginning. Then, turning back to David's father, he said, 'How long do you expect the work to take?'

'It's hard to be precise. We have seven volunteers starting tomorrow, and we have the assistance of the local archaeological society in the evenings and at weekends. But time is always the great problem with these rescue digs. We don't yet know how long they're prepared to hold up work on the motorway.'

The man nodded sympathetically. 'I imagine they rate the motorway as considerably more important than your work,' he said. 'This must be a very pleasant assignment for you. Most excavation is destruction, wouldn't you agree? You dig your way down through the strata and anything you miss – or misinterpret – is lost for ever. But uncovering a work of art must be most satisfying.'

He seemed oblivious to the expression on Professor Birch's face, but something in his manner made David suspect he was being deliberately mischievous.

Then he became a little more serious. 'Do you have any ideas about the subject of the mosaic?' he said.

'All that can be said at the moment is that it is large and that the tiny portions that have been revealed are in a surprisingly good condition,' said Professor Birch in his reporter-manner. He divided people into two clear departments – 'reporter-types', who were either actual reporters or else passers-by who asked questions automatically without really caring to know the answers, and 'real people'. With real people he would sometimes permit a little warmth to creep into his manner.

'I would like to go on record,' said the man cheerfully, 'for saying that the mosaic will depict Diana, the Roman goddess of the moon.'

For the moment the Professor showed a spark of interest. 'You've found a reference?' he said.

'No. But this whole area belongs to the moon.'

The spark died. 'I'll remember what you've said. And now, if you'll excuse me . . .'

The man nodded, and smiled, but did not move, which meant that David's father had to walk away from him, crossing a patch of muddy ground to peer intently at an area he had not particularly wanted to investigate at that moment.

David stood a little uncertainly, looking from one to the other, then he wandered over to join his father who was crouching down and stabbing at the ground with his forefinger. 'One of these cranks who thinks he knows more about a subject than people who've studied it for years,' he was grumbling into the earth.

'Why don't you have him to help you?' said David, knowing the answer but wanting to hear it.

'I've got work to do,' said his father. 'I can't cope with some elderly hippie at the same time. We'd better get back. I should think that woman probably serves lunch on the dot.'

'Mrs Foster,' said David automatically. His father rarely remembered names from the present century. He looked around. The man had disappeared and the huge mound of earth and rubble, and the great, scarred, scraped area that formed the site, suddenly looked indescribably bleak. He realized he was either depressed or hungry. Probably both.

'All right,' he said.

Each maintained his silence until they were almost at the small, grey house where Mrs Foster did bed and breakfast, with extra meals on request.

'How did you get on?' said David, then.

'All right,' said his father. 'How about you?'

'All right.'

In the hallway the smell of food competed with the strangely dry and dusty smell of caged birds. They walked into the small dining-room, expecting to be the only guests, as they had been at breakfast. But seated at the second table, viewing the two lethargic budgerigars with apparent interest, was the Professor's elderly hippie.

'Hallo again,' he said with great pleasure. 'It seems we're neighbours.'

Professor Birch hesitated in the doorway, with David crowding into his back, then strode purposefully to his own table, sitting with his back to the other man. 'Yes, indeed,' he said.

'My name's John Westwood, and I know you're Professor Birch because I read about you in the local paper.'

'How do you do,' said the Professor, seeming to address himself to the food which had just arrived in front of him.

No one said much until the meal was over. Mrs Foster cleared the tables, set a mug of tea in front of each of them and went away again.

By that stage the silence, broken only by the rasping of one budgerigar's beak on its cuttlefish, no longer seemed quite proper to David. He glanced over at Mr Westwood to find that the man was looking at him in quite a friendly way.

'Do you spend a lot of time looking at archaeological sites?' said David tentatively.

Mr Westwood seemed more than ready to talk.

'I spend nearly all my time reading,' he said. 'Although I always try to link my study to a particular focal point. As a matter of fact, I'm rather more interested in the stone circle up on the moor than in your father's dig.'

'So am I,' said David. There were several things he wanted to add, but he played safe. 'What do you read?'

'Archaeology, astrology, astronomy, geology, geography, prehistory, mythology, folklore, mathematics and geometry. All very relevant to the problem in hand, and each one worthy of a lifetime's study.'

David eyed him thoughtfully. 'All that – to understand the circle?' he said.

'Did you think it could be understood with less?'

'But how do you have time to learn so much?'

'I shall have all the time I need. No man dies before he has finished what he came to do.'

David's father huffed loudly. 'I don't think that's strictly true,' he said.

'Oh, but it is,' said Mr Westwood, laughing. 'If I die before I've finished, it will mean that this was not my work – I took a wrong turning. But I don't believe that, I believe I'm on the right lines.'

'What about the economics of the thing?' said the Professor. 'Do you not have to spend some small part of your life earning a living?'

'I don't have time to go to work,' said Mr Westwood. 'Sadly, no one is prepared to pay for my researches – the way they pay for yours, Professor. However, I'm lucky enough to have a small private income which is sufficient for my frugal standard of living.'

'So in effect you have become a full-time student for the rest of your life with no end or job in view?' said Professor Birch.

'I don't have a material end in view. But it's not essential to measure every activity in terms of possible financial reward, you know.'

'It would be very nice if one didn't have to,' said Professor Birch. 'But in my own particular case I have a wife and a son to keep.'

'Ah well – in *my* own particular case I have no children and my wife left me years ago. So I have no responsibilities.'

The Professor rose from the table. 'If you will excuse me, I must go to my room and make some notes,' he said.

When he had gone, David said, 'He doesn't really mean to be rude.' Then he added, 'Why *all* those subjects?'

'If I know nothing of astrology and astronomy, how can I hope to discover whether or not certain circles were designed to study the sky, to predict eclipses, to draw energy from particular configurations of the stars overhead? I need some understanding of geography if I am to know why the circles are placed where they are, in relation to the earth as well as in relation to the sky. Archaeology and prehistory are obviously necessary, and mathematics and geometry help me to appreciate with what precision the circle-makers worked. All vital, you will agree?'

'And you said geology?'

'Come now – that's obvious, surely. You can't study a structure without understanding something about the materials it is made from. It may be that the circle-makers chose special stone for their work, and if that is so I would like to be in a position to appreciate the fact. After all, we know that the stone for the great monument we call Stonehenge came all the way from the Prescelli mountains in Wales. Perhaps any old stone won't do for these structures – any more than any old ore will serve in place of uranium.'

'My father says . . .' David began, then hesitated.

'I should like to hear what your father says,' Mr Westwood prompted.

'Well – he says that he agrees that the stone for Stonehenge came from the Prescelli mountains, but he doesn't believe men brought it all those miles on purpose. He says Stonehenge is built from glacial erratics. He says the ice brought the stone – and when the ice melted and men moved into the area and began to create things, they used the stone they found. They didn't know or care where it came from. They used it because it was there.'

'I've heard that theory, too,' said Mr Westwood. 'It may be correct – and it may not. Perhaps the truth is somewhere between the two. Perhaps the only suitable stones were brought by chance to the place where they were needed. I still believe it is important for me to have a good working knowledge of geology.'

'So you read all you can on all those subjects?'

'You make it sound a little haphazard. It isn't. I've

23

mapped out a course of study for myself – allowing a little time off to examine specific structures, of course. Otherwise I might begin to study for study's own sake and forget the purpose.'

'A one-man university?'

'Yes. I'm half-way through my fifth year.'

'A five-year course? That's long.'

'No. A twelve-year course. Just to begin with.'

'Twelve years!' said David. 'Full time!' He shook some salt on to the tablecloth and rubbed his forefinger over its pleasant grittiness. 'I don't think I can imagine committing myself for twelve years.'

'Then you're not as interested in circles as you think you are.'

Although said without any viciousness at all, the remark came out like a blow. Still apparently busy with the salt, David sought to deflect it.

'And mythology? You said mythology.'

'Mythology and local folklore are very important. Within the most fantastic legends there is usually, perhaps always, a kernel of truth. The story of an actual event is often passed down the years, gathering layers of embroidery and confusion on the way. If you are studying a particular area, every local legend is relevant. So long as you can get behind the legend to the facts.'

David wanted to say that getting behind legends interested him, too, but he was afraid it might sound ingratiating.

'You said to my father that the area belonged to the moon. Was it legends that told you that?'

'No. That was instinct and dowsing.'

'You dowse for water, don't you?' said David, imagining forked hazel twigs and underground springs.

'You can dowse for anything.' From his jacket-pocket Mr Westwood produced a small and beautifully polished wooden ball suspended from a length of strong twine with a knot at the end. He took the knot between finger and thumb and held the small pendulum out to David.

'Perfectly balanced,' he said. 'I made it myself.'

'What does it find?' said David.

'What I'm looking for. If it's there, that is.'

'How?'

'A circular movement is a positive – a "yes" – a to-and-fro movement is a negative – a "no". I ask questions and I get answers.'

David picked at his thumbnail. 'Well,' he said doubtfully, 'we had things like that at school once. They came in Christmas crackers. Little bits of brass-coloured metal on the end of red woolly cotton. They worked like you said, and you were supposed to be able to tell if a person was lying or not.'

'That's right,' said Westwood unperturbed, putting the pendulum back in his pocket since David didn't seem disposed to take it from him. 'A crude form of the same thing.'

David continued to pick at his nail.

Westwood laughed. 'It shouldn't worry you,' he said. 'When you were small you probably had a toy gun and a Mickey Mouse watch. I presume that hasn't made you doubt the effectiveness of real guns and real watches.'

'Did you come here specially to see this circle?'

'Yes, I did.'

'Why this one?'

'I'm making a study of stone circles and this one interested me particularly. For one thing it's a very fine example, pretty well complete. For another, it's extremely easy to reach from this town. I don't have to spend half a day hiking out to it and half a day hiking back again. And then, of course, this is the correct time of year.'

'How do you mean?'

'The circle belongs to the moon – and this time of year is governed by Cancer – the Crab – the moon's sign.'

David pondered on the information in silence for a moment. 'I'm interested in stone circles, too,' he said at last. 'But I only came here because my father is working on the dig. I was just lucky there was a circle near by.'

'We can join forces and pool our information, if you like,' said Mr Westwood.

David was so utterly taken aback by the offer that he just stared, trying to work out whether Mr Westwood was incredibly generous or whether he was under the mistaken impression that David had some useful store of information.

'I expect you'd rather work on your own,' said Mr Westwood, easily, filling the amazed silence before it grew too long. 'But if I can help . . . There should never be any rivalry in this sort of thing, you know.'

FOUR

On Monday, when he judged school would be out, David made his way down to the bridge again. He could see from some way off that the two figures were below the mill, just as Tim had promised they would be. He walked along the river's edge to join them.

They all nodded rather formally to each other and nobody said anything for a while.

Then, 'How's it going?' said David.

This time Jane was making the notes and Tim was gazing rather despondently into the water.

'Not so good,' he said. And, after a pause, 'the river's running too high.'

'How do you mean?' said David.

Tim looked steadily at him and then away again. 'It's as high now as it ever is,' he said. 'And it shouldn't be at this time of year.'

'It's all this rain,' said David. 'There must be a lot of water coming down from the hills.'

'Give that man an Oscar,' said Tim. 'Nobel prize and bar.'

'Well, that's what it *is*,' said David indignantly. 'I don't see why it should surprise you so much.'

'I know what it *is*,' said Tim. 'It just makes it a bit difficult, that's all.'

'In what way?' said David.

'The river's high and flowing very fast.'

'I see that,' said David with exaggerated patience. 'But what effect does that have on your survey?'

'Quite a lot,' said Tim, and reached out his hand for the notes. Jane passed them to him, and then sat gazing at the river and rubbing the side of her neck.

David gave up and sat down on the damp river bank.

'I've been to the library today,' he said, mostly to Jane. 'I've been trying to find out about the stone circle, but nobody seems to have written about it. If it's ever been excavated, there's no record. All I could find were two legends.'

Tim handed the notes back to Jane. 'We might as well give up,' he said. 'We're not going to get much here.' Then, to David, 'Our Mam says you can come to tea tomorrow if you want. You can see what we've done on the pollution survey.'

David was rather touched that they had been sufficiently aware of his presence to mention him at home.

'Thanks,' he said. 'What time?'

'Meet you on the bridge about half five,' said Tim. 'We live over there.' He waved his arm in an arc that included the entire town.

'Thanks,' said David again. 'Look, do you want to hear about these legends, or do you know about them already?'

'I didn't think it was legends you were after,' said Tim. 'What with your Dad being an archaeologist, I thought it would be facts.'

28

'Well if something is as obscure as that circle,' said David, 'you just have to collect everything you possibly can. I've got two legends and the map reference so far.'

For a moment he was tempted to deliver a short lecture on the truth hidden within fantasies, but the moment passed. He saw that Tim was unlikely to be interested in the symbolism of Sleeping Beauty – or the mystery of 'fairy food', the food which no human can eat and retain his freedom. So he just pulled his notebook out of his hip pocket, which was where his father always kept his notes, and doggedly passed on the information he had collected, whether they wanted it or not.

'They were in two different books,' he said. 'I didn't write out the first one in full, I just took notes. Apparently, in "high summer", whenever that is, the stones are supposed to come down at midnight to drink from this river. The second story I did write out. It says, "Concerning the Weeping Stones it is said that once, long ago, Midsummer Night fell on a Saturday. The young men and girls from the village went out on to the hillside to dance hand in hand in a circle and celebrate this event or, some say, to carry out a pagan ceremony. They were warned by the elders of the village to stop their dance at midnight because dancing on the Sabbath was not permitted. However, they became so carried away that they danced right through until dawn, at which moment they were turned into stone as a punishment. Each year, on the anniversary of the event, the stones weep for their sins." Nice, isn't it?' He looked up at them.

Jane was watching the water a little wistfully. David

29

felt the stories had caught her imagination but he suddenly knew he couldn't be bothered to try and nag a response out of her.

Tim just shrugged. 'The stories are OK,' he said, 'but they're not much use are they? The first one's rubbish. And the second one just explains the name.'

'I'm not saying,' said David, 'that people were turned to stone, or that the stones ever move. I'm only saying I think the legends are interesting. You see, the funny thing is, I've come across them both before. I've only ever seen two other stone circles in all my life and each of them had both these stories – almost word for word, except for the name. Don't you think that's strange?'

'No,' said Tim. 'We had a supply teacher for a term last year and he was going all over the country collecting legends. He'd been to all kinds of places, but he'd only got about four stories. He kept finding the same ones.'

'But that doesn't make the stories any less interesting,' said David. 'OK, I accept that the second one evolved to explain the name, but in that case where did the name Weeping Stones come from in the first place?'

Tim shrugged. 'Maybe they invented the story to explain the circle, then, and the name came from the story. The point is the story is as unconnected to the stones as if you yourself personally sat down and made up a fairy tale about how and why York Minster was built.'

David was silenced for a moment, partly because he had never expected to hear Tim talk so much. 'I still think,' he said at last, 'that if you're investigating something you have to make a note of everything connected with it, however fantastic.'

'Fair enough,' said Tim.

'I'm going to the local archaeological society next,' said David, feeling that his methods of research had been discredited. 'That's definitely the next step.'

'Been up to the circle again, have you?' said Tim.

'Yes, this morning,' said David. 'Nothing happened.' He didn't add that he had only gone as far as the final ridge, looked at the stones from several yards away, and hurried straight down again. It had struck him then that they were like stones dropped in water – the circle of their presence seemed to widen like a ripple and push him back.

'You're putting Baby Jane's nose out of joint,' said Tim. 'She thinks the stones are hers, and now there's some arty old bloke wandering around checking up on them, as well as you.'

'Oh, I bet I know who that is,' said David. 'His name's John Westwood and he's staying where we are. Did he ask you about the stones?'

'Yes.'

'What did you tell him?'

'Same as I told you.'

'What did you think of him?'

'Not much. No, he was all right, I suppose.'

'I'm sorry if you feel strangers are butting in,' said David to Jane. 'Can't we all join forces?'

'I'm not bothered,' said Jane.

David relapsed into silence again. It seemed almost

impossible to get through to either of them. He felt as if there was an enormous reservoir of questions and answers and ideas within each of them, but that he somehow couldn't tap it.

Jane tilted her head to the right and ran her hand up and down the left side of her neck.

'Have you got lice, or what?' said Tim suddenly, quite sharply, without even looking at her.

'It's all these peas in my neck,' said Jane dreamily.

'Peas?'

'Lumps. All up the sides of my neck.'

'Don't worry, I expect you've just got swine fever.' Tim looked at David and then back at Jane. 'The hypochondriac in its natural habitat,' he said.

'Explain what you meant about the high water being a nuisance,' said David, firmly.

'Well,' said Tim, 'it changes everything.'

All at once Jane exploded into giggles, and her giggles seemed to release her from her withdrawn state.

'He thinks he's told you all about it already,' she said. 'If he *thinks* it he thinks he's *said* it. It's only that we're trying to double-check our last survey. We know the mill affects the water because we've found less water-life below it than above it. But last time we looked there was lots of dye below the mill and we were going to take photographs and samples. But now the river is so high and fast it's washed all the dye away.'

'Rocks there,' said Tim, waving at the water, 'were covered in slippery, purple-coloured stuff.'

'What rocks?' said David.

'That's just it,' said Tim gloomily. 'What rocks! They're under water now.'

'But you mean you know that the mill does cause pollution?' said David.

'Oh yes.'

'What are you going to do about it?'

'We-e-ell,' said Tim.

'But it's important, isn't it?' said David.

'Quite minor, compared with some things that go on in this country,' said Tim.

'It may be minor, but it all adds to the trouble, doesn't it?'

'Yes.'

'Well when they told you to do the survey, at school, what did they say you had to do when you'd finished? Present the results to them, or what?'

'Not really,' said Tim. 'We're supposed to do something ourselves.'

'Well – like what?'

Tim shrugged.

David looked at Jane.

'We're supposed to go and see someone about it,' she said. 'I mean – our survey being the mill – we're really supposed to see the foreman and prove to him the mill is damaging the life in the river and ask him to see if anything can be done about it.'

'And are you going to do that?' said David.

'I want to get this double-check out of the way first,' said Tim.

'You said you already knew it was causing pollution.'

'Yes.'

'Well then you must go and see the foreman. I mean – pollution – it concerns everybody, doesn't it? Everybody's got to do something. And it's perfectly obvious what your part is. You have to tell the foreman his mill is discharging a lot of dye into the water and it's a bad thing.'

'Dye and wool grease,' said Tim sadly.

'Must be quite easy to find out who the foreman is,' said David. 'I'll come with you if you like. Can I come with you?'

'We'll wait and see,' said Tim. 'I'd like to have another shot at this survey first.'

David exploded with long pent-up irritation. Forgetting that he hardly knew Tim, he began to shout at him. 'Why won't you *do* something?' and he actually hit the river bank with the flat of his hand, something he had never thought to see himself do. 'You know exactly what to do and you're just putting it off. My father won't even use bleached lavatory paper because the chemicals cause pollution. Why are you so apathetic?'

Tim turned his head and looked at him stolidly. 'I don't much care if your Dad uses old fish-and-chip papers,' he said. 'I got to be careful. My Dad works at the mill.'

FIVE

It was the middle house of a low, grey terrace. David pressed the bell and then, because it didn't seem to ring, knocked on the panels of the door. He heard quick, light footsteps and the door was opened by a small, fat man with tiny hands and feet. 'All right, all right,' he said. 'Ringing and banging! What's so urgent?'

'I'm sorry,' said David. 'I didn't hear the bell.'

'No. You're not meant to. I'm the one who has to hear it. I'm the one who has to answer it. Well then? What's the problem?'

'Mr Thatcher?'

'Yes?'

'Is it right that you're the president of the local archaeological society?'

'Yes, it is right.'

'I'm trying to find out something about the Weeping Stones. I wondered if you could help me – or is this an inconvenient time?'

'You're not local, are you?'

'No – actually, I'm Professor Birch's son.'

'Oh *are* you?' said Mr Thatcher, his whole manner changing. 'Come in, won't you. You're here on the dig, I take it? As a matter of fact I shall be going down there myself in about half an hour. Of course one should be at work, but all this is far too important to miss.'

He led David into the front room, which was set up as an office. It was a small room made smaller by a large green filing-cabinet which stood in one corner with its drawers slightly open, a huge, curved desk that had been designed for a large office and, jammed in between the two, a tall wardrobe with doors ajar, inside which sagging home-made shelves supported stacks of papers. The only wall that was not busy with door, or window, or wardrobe and filing-cabinet, was covered with maps and charts of the area.

'Come in,' said Mr Thatcher again, 'and I'll show you one or two things you might be interested in.'

The room was so small that David rather felt they should take turns to stand in it. There was a very faint smell of mouldy cheese which he at first took to be characteristic of amateur archaeology until he noticed a cheese sandwich, long forgotten, on the filing-cabinet.

'Of course, I was first on the scene when the workmen revealed part of the mosaic,' said Mr Thatcher without pause. 'I'd been watching down there off and on for quite a time. I knew they'd find something. I've always been quite certain there was a very important villa in just that area. My researches have been pointing that way for years. All the supportive evidence for my ideas is in this room, as I told your father. Unfortunately he hasn't had a moment to come and look through it yet. But one can only dig in daylight and I'm sure that before the season is over he'll find an evening . . .'

'The evenings are light quite late at this time of year

– and he has to write up his notes . . .' said David, automatically protective. 'But I'm not really interested in the mosaic – I'm trying to do some research on the stone circle. Do you have anything on that?'

'Of course, the circle is up on the moors and off the beaten track – and I mean that quite literally,' said Mr Thatcher dismissively. 'But for years I've been finding evidence of an important Roman road which we now know leads to the mosaic. Look, look here.'

There seemed no way to avoid being shown the rather pathetic haul of trophies – a few unspectacular Roman coins, each mounted on a large piece of card, and a ring, believed to be iron-age. David grew weary of hearing under which house, or beside which cable or pipelaying operation, each had been found, and of looking at a map on which had been marked, in dotted lines, what Mr Thatcher believed to be the course of a Roman road, indicated by these finds.

All the time, Mr Thatcher talked on. 'I keep an eye open for any kind of digging work going on in the area,' he said, 'and as soon as they reach maximum depth I nip down and grub around for a while. The workmen are always most understanding – they don't mind at all. I always find some little thing – though never before anything that warranted a complete excavation. When I do find something I gather the men around me and give them a little lecture on it. After all, it's only due to their cooperation that I'm able to find these things in the first place – and they're always most gratifyingly interested.'

David pictured the irritation and boredom of the

workmen and mentally gave them a gold star for humouring Mr Thatcher. Then, with a slight shock, he thought, whose side am I on? I'm one of the ones who believe it's vital to find and examine everything. I should be impressed.

'Of course we now know for certain that I'm right, there *was* a road,' Thatcher was saying, 'because the mosaic points to the presence of an important villa and there must have been an access road. However, as your father so rightly says, it's unlikely that we'd get funds to dig for the road itself . . .'

The minute room seemed to be getting smaller by the moment, and David caught himself seriously wondering if it held enough air for both of them. He didn't feel he could endure very much more of Mr Thatcher's eager hospitality.

He tried one more time. 'Do you have any information on the stone circle?' he said.

Mr Thatcher looked at him for a moment or two with a faintly puzzled air. Then, 'No,' he said, simply.

SIX

In the front room the table was laid for tea – buttered buns, small chocolate cakes, a bowlful of tinned peaches and, at each place, a plateful of ham and salad. On stools by the hearth Jane, Tim and David worked their way through the notes on the pollution survey and in the kitchen Mrs Thornby buttered bread and waited for the kettle to boil and Mr Thornby to come home.

Seeing the results of the pollution survey on paper, when he had already been told them verbally, was not actually very exciting, for all that Tim was good at drawing mayfly larvae. David was in any case rather fed up with admiring other people's projects, so he was quite relieved when the back door slammed and Tim said, 'There's our Dad.'

The door between the front room and the kitchen was slightly ajar so they could hear quite clearly when Tim's father said, 'We're going on to overtime.'

'That'll put him in a good mood,' said Tim quietly.

'He doesn't sound very pleased,' David whispered back.

'He never does sound pleased, but he will be, inside.'

'Why overtime, then?' said Mrs Thornby.

Mr Thornby seemed to be splashing about in the sink. 'Put in a tender for a big order and won, that's why,' he said. 'Beat Harrisons over the way and they're twice our size. But the delivery date's tight and we'll have to keep the machines going round the clock. Means shift work and overtime.'

'Well!' said Mrs Thornby. 'There'll be a fatter pay packet, then.'

'There will. Good job we had the new plant and generator put in when we did. Otherwise we'd never do it.'

'Then that's very nice,' said Mrs Thornby. 'Come and meet our guest.'

Mr Thornby came into the front room carrying the bread and butter and the teapot, and Mrs Thornby followed him carrying a saucepanful of hot baked beans. She ladled some on to each plate, beside the ham. 'Don't wait,' she said to David, 'or they'll all be done before you begin. Oh, and Jane, love, I've booked your dentist appointment. He'll see you next Saturday morning.'

'But that's the eighth,' said Jane. 'That's my birthday.'

'Well if it hurts as much as you say, you'll be glad to go and get it done. I tried to make it sooner, but he's that booked up. It seems everyone's having trouble right now.'

'All right,' said Jane.

'It's all this fancy sweet stuff,' said her father quite suddenly. He shoved at the plateful of cakes. 'Didn't have all this stuff when I was young – couldn't afford it. *And* we were none the worse for the loss.'

'Ah, now, be fair, Jane doesn't eat much sweet stuff. Just cakes at special teas, that's all,' said her mother. 'Never mind, lovey, at least your birthday's on a Saturday this year – you don't have to go to school.'

Mr Thornby, having entered into the conversation, seemed all at once very alert.

'Have you left school?' he said to David.

'No.'

'Then why aren't you at school now? Holidays haven't begun.'

'It's nearly the end of term,' said David. 'My father wanted me to come with him on the dig.'

'So he took you out of school, is that it? Can he do that? Is it allowed?'

'They don't mind . . . as long as he keeps paying the fees . . .'

Mr Thornby watched him through the steam that rose from his baked beans. 'It's *that* sort of school, is it?' he said.

David breathed in and then out again. 'My father thinks I'll probably learn more coming on the dig than I would from books,' he said.

Mr Thornby relaxed. 'Happen he may very well be right,' he said, and got on with his tea.

The atmosphere seemed to become easier until Tim suddenly said, 'I can see you letting me off school to give more time to the pollution survey.'

'Grubbing about in the mud at your age,' said Mr Thornby.

Tim clattered his knife and fork down on to his plate and Mrs Thornby spread a quick smile across her face and said, 'Now, now. Let's get through tea in peace for once.'

'Well what's his Dad doing,' Tim demanded at exactly the same time, 'but grubbing about in the mud at *your* age?'

'It's a job – being an archaeologist – isn't it?' said Mr Thornby. 'Perhaps this lad wants to do the same thing when he starts work.'

'And you don't think there are any worthwhile jobs connected with ecology?'

'Not with your education.'

Mrs Thornby tried to cut in just before the next major explosion, but nobody took any notice of her except Jane, who half smiled and offered her a cake.

'Well my education isn't my fault right now,' said Tim. 'But when I leave school I'm going to find a way to earn money *and* go on studying, and I'm going to *do* something . . .'

'I know what you're going to do,' said Mr Thornby. 'You're going to end up the oldest schoolboy in the business.'

'Why is it all right for him,' said Tim, slowly and much too loudly, jabbing his forefinger into David's shoulder, 'and not all right for me?'

'Now then,' said Mrs Thornby. 'David's our guest. Let's not have one of your great argy-bargies.'

'It's not mine,' said Tim, 'it's Dad's – he started it. *And* that's just it, isn't it? David's a guest so nobody's going to say they know archaeology's a useless occupation – but it's perfectly all right to say that what I want to do is useless – when what I want to do would be really practical.'

42

'Why do you think archaeology is useless?' said David, politely and very mildly, hoping to put some kind of dampener on the conflict.

Tim continued to glare at his father for a moment, but Mr Thornby was finishing his food and taking no notice of anybody.

Tim turned slowly and rather irritably back to David. 'It's just holding up the motorway,' he said.

'Motorways destroy natural habitats and bring petrol fumes,' said David. 'So isn't a hold-up a good thing?'

'I doubt if the men who've been laid off on half-pay think that,' said Tim.

'No – I'm interested,' said David carefully. 'I'm interested in your views because – well – the stone circle – I mean, I know a lot of people aren't impressed by it, but I'm *so* impressed by it that I can't understand anyone else not being. So, for instance, why aren't you?'

Tim sighed, picked up his knife and fork, shovelled down the last mouthful and pushed his plate away from him.

'Well – it's dead, isn't it?'

'Dead?'

'What else? It doesn't *do* anything. It isn't for people now. I'm not saying it wasn't very important when it was put up – I'm sure it must have been – but it isn't now. The motorway is what's important now.'

There seemed no answer to that and David kept quiet, seeing the sense of what had been said and at the same time wondering how something dead could exert so much power.

'There's a lot of talk about this Westwood man in the town,' said Tim's father unexpectedly. 'Is he working with your father?'

'Oh no,' said David.

'Bit of a weirdo by all accounts,' said Mr Thornby.

'I wouldn't say that,' said David.

'You know him, do you?'

'He's staying where we are.'

'Which one's the typical archaeologist, then, him or your father?'

Apparently Mrs Thornby sensed the aggression mounting again because she said, 'Now let's all stop talking about archaeology and weirdos and everything else. We've got to decide whether Jane's having a surprise for her birthday or whether she wants to choose something. Now, have you thought about it, love?'

That night, David stood at the window of his attic bedroom. The moon, though not yet full, was quite bright and the misting rain had stopped for the first time since they arrived. He had a glimpse between rooftops of the river, gleaming and seemingly still. He raised his father's binoculars to his eyes and looked towards the undulation on the moor, beyond the river, where the circle stood. Although he had hoped to focus on it he was surprised, almost shocked, to find that he could. It belonged to that world, out there, and it was strange to look at it from between Mrs Foster's chintzy curtains.

The stones looked remote, distant and ill-defined. Then, as he watched, something vague and unidentifiable

44

began to flit past them . . . Round and round the stones
it went, so that they seemed to flicker as it passed between
each one and the moonlight. Round and round, slowly
and rhythmically . . .

SEVEN

It was still very early. The sun was pale and weak but the stones shone with moisture. Each tiny unevenness of the surface threw its own tiny shadow. The stones looked at once more solid and more vulnerable than they ever had before.

David was breathing heavily from his climb. A tall shabby figure with thin grey hair trailing over his shoulders was standing just outside the ring. It was Mr Westwood – busy packing away a tripod and some kind of instrument. He looked up and smiled.

'Have you been here all night?' said David.

'Yes. Their time is very close.'

David's scalp prickled. 'What's happening?'

'I'm not sure yet. It has to do with water and the moon.'

'How can you tell?'

'In many ways. The name indicates a connection with water.'

'Weeping Stones? But the name must be far newer than the circle.'

'That doesn't matter. The spirit of this place has always existed. When symbols, and later words, came into use it would naturally attract the relevant ones.'

'You say their time is close . . . as if they're going to give birth . . .'

'Something like that, yes.'

They were outside the circle, Mr Westwood to the left, next to the two tall gate stones, and David in front so that the circle was partly skylined for him and seemed to look down on him from its superior position.

David felt that they were conducting a very delicate conversation – that one wrong word would destroy the structure which would collapse and bury its valuables.

'It's as if the stones are conscious,' he said slowly. 'But even when they frighten me I don't really believe that.'

'The air trapped inside a balloon is no different to the air outside it,' said Mr Westwood. 'Consciousness is everywhere. But here "conscious" is the wrong word, the wrong concept. Rather they are active. They have been activated.'

'I saw movement up here in the moonlight,' said David. 'Was it you?'

'I was here.'

'I half thought something was dancing round the circle.'

'Water and the moon,' said Mr Westwood. 'The undines were here – are here.'

'Undines?'

'Water elementals. Who can move in water, or in mist, or in mist upon water.'

The sun was collecting the mist, not dispersing it. Soon the mist and dampness would win and the day would be as grey and moist as the day before and the day before that.

David felt as if his blood was full of tiny windchimes, vibrating on a high clear note.

'You mean "fairies"?'

'In a way.'

David half laughed. 'I don't believe in fairies.'

'You don't believe in pseudo-fairies who wear pointed shoes and wave tinsel wands. You believe in the spirit of this place.'

The centre of the circle gleamed with moisture, almost as if a pond were forming. The minute shadows died among the grain of the stones.

If fairies were spirits of place their existence all at once seemed certain. 'So bad fairies live in bad areas?' he said.

'Yes. Harsh and demanding fairies in the hard and rough areas of Scotland and Wales. Generous fairies in the rich, easy farmlands down south. Capricious fairies lead men to their deaths in fens and marshes. Every narrow strait, every whirlpool, every deep lake, once had its named spirit whom children were taught to fear.'

'Instead of saying, "That lake is deep, you could drown in it", people said, "Keep away or the monster will get you"?'

'Right.'

David's excitement rose. 'And most fairies, if travellers respect them, will guide them safely – which only means that if you respect the dangers of a place and behave sensibly you'll probably survive?'

'Just that. Although I prefer the originals to the interpretations. It should be possible to understand these things without taking all the magic out of them.'

'I'm sorry,' said David, and he knew he had destroyed the mood. 'But it's new to me. I wonder where that puts the idea of fairy food?'

Mr Westwood looked at him without comment. David saw that he was damp all over, as damp as the ground and the stones and the air. His thick sweater and corduroy jeans seemed to be designed to retain rather than to repel moisture.

David pursued his thought aloud but alone. 'In so many of the stories, a person is told that if he goes into the world of the fairies he mustn't eat or drink anything or he'll crave more and more of the food and be bound to the fairies for ever and pine away . . .'

'I need some food of a rather coarser kind,' said Mr Westwood, turning away. 'Mrs Foster won't serve breakfast for some time yet. I think I'll go to the café by the square. Will you join me?'

David felt safer within the stones' sphere now that Mr Westwood was there, and didn't want to leave them. But he didn't want to leave Mr Westwood, either, so he agreed.

'It must have been cold up here last night,' he said.

'Cool and damp. What I need now is a brisk walk and a cup of tea.'

As they left the stones further and further behind them David began to feel a sense of elation which he presumed had to do with the earliness of the hour and Mr Westwood's company.

'What's that you're carrying?' he asked.

'A theodolite. I've been taking some measurements.'

'If I'd come up even earlier you could have shown me how to use one,' said David. 'I shall have to know, if I'm going to do anything serious about stone circles.'

'It might take a while to initiate you.'

'You don't mind me asking?'

'I'm delighted to help, I told you that. I'd also like to have a hand in the books you read. *You* won't be offended if I make out a list?'

'Would you?' said David.

'I'll let you have it in a couple of days.'

David laughed.

'What's funny?' said Mr Westwood.

'It's just that I feel very cheerful today,' said David, striding down the slope beside him, 'and I feel like running but my shoes have collected so much clay I can hardly pick my feet up.'

They reached the road. 'Look,' he said, holding a monstrous shoe out for inspection. 'It's so sticky I can hardly bang it free.'

At the bridge they met Jane and Tim crossing from the other side.

'You're early,' said David.

'Taking a look at the river before school,' said Tim.

'It doesn't look any different,' said David, scraping his feet more or less clean on the side of the bridge. 'Come to the café with us instead.'

He was a little surprised at his own bossiness, especially as the other two fell into step quite meekly, but Mr Westwood seemed happy about it. The delicate mood at the circle, when the air had seemed pregnant with revelations only to be reached by very precise steps, had long passed, and suddenly Mr Westwood was everyone's favourite uncle, ushering them into the empty café and ordering egg on toast and tea all round.

The café-owner, although he nodded a greeting to Jane and Tim, seemed cross – probably because he was the only one on duty and had to cook the breakfasts himself, David thought. He banged the cups of tea down so hard that waves slopped to and fro for long seconds, but Mr Westwood made no comment.

'I went up to the stones this morning,' said David, chattily, 'and found he'd been up there all night.' He was at once aware that this struck a false note with Jane, although she said nothing.

'Are you going to excavate?' said Tim to Mr Westwood, without any real interest.

'No, that isn't how you work, is it?' said David.

'What then?' said Tim.

Mr Westwood didn't offer any information and David, although too elated to keep his mouth shut out of respect, found it difficult to word a really satisfactory answer.

'It's to do with water and the moon,' he said. 'To do with astrology.'

'I wouldn't want to know the future,' said Jane rather sadly. 'In case it was bad.'

David, who didn't much care which way the conversation went so long as he was in on it, began to say something rather hearty about the future perhaps being even better than the present, but Mr Westwood overrode him.

'It's given to very few to know the future,' he said.

'But astrology tells you the future,' said Tim.

'No good astrologer will tell you the future. As soon as anyone says "I see happiness, nine sons and a long voyage" you must be wary.'

'Then what does astrology tell you?' said Tim, and for once he actually looked as if he wanted an answer.

'On a personal level, it can tell you about yourself.'

'That's dull. I know about myself.'

'Wonderful. I congratulate you. It's a rare person who can make such a statement.'

Tim was not crushed. 'I know what I'm like,' he persisted. 'And I know what all these palmists and gipsies tell people they're like. *She's* been to some and they all said she was sensitive and artistic. Exactly what she wanted to hear.'

Jane slid back her chair and turned a thunderous face towards the door.

'Stay!' said Mr Westwood, quite sharply for him. 'Stay and face it out.'

Jane cast him a quick look from under her hair and remained where she was, but sitting sideways on to the table.

Mr Westwood turned his attention back to Tim. 'I'm not talking about seaside fortune-tellers who know what's wanted and supply it,' he said. 'I'm talking about people who interpret a horoscope and explain your nature to you. Those who can tell you where your talents lie so that you know in which field you are likely to be successful and happy. Those who can tell you your faults and weaknesses so that you know what you have to fight against.'

'There's no point,' said Tim. 'You are the way you are. There's nothing can change it.'

'Not so,' said Mr Westwood. 'Paracelsus said, "Man's wisdom is in no way subjugated, and is no one's slave . . . therefore the stars must obey man and be subject to him and not he to the stars. Even if he is a child of Saturn and if Saturn has overshadowed his birth, he can master Saturn and become a child of the sun".'

Tim gazed long and steadily at Mr Westwood. 'Well, who was Para – whatyousaid?'

'A renaissance alchemist,' said Mr Westwood with a certain mischievous amusement creeping into his eyes. 'As a matter of fact, Paracelsus wasn't his real name – would you like his real name? It was Theophrastus Bombastus von Hohenheim. Para-whatIsaid is easier.'

'Well – what's it supposed to mean if you're a "child of Saturn"?'

'Saturn is the greater malefic.'

'What does *that* mean?'

'It means that in many traditions the planet Saturn is seen as a baleful influence, a bringer of harm and limitation. Though of course a well-aspected Saturn can be very beneficial indeed.'

'You're making all this up,' said Tim irritably.

'No, I'm not. I'm only trying to point out that you can overcome almost anything in your nature – if you understand the problem. Suppose, for instance, that Jane was told that she sees competition and hostility where there are none – that she defends herself against attacks that have not been, and never will be, made – then she could begin to control her own unhappy feelings.'

Somehow unable to leave the table, Jane resorted to the only other defence she knew. She turned her head slowly towards Mr Westwood, dragging her eyes with apparent effort away from the wall poster she had been looking at, and said 'What?' as if she hadn't heard a word for the past several minutes.

Mr Westwood ignored her.

'You should be able to work those things out for yourself,' said Tim.

'You can. But it isn't easy and it takes time.'

'We're going to be late for school,' said Jane, suddenly, truthfully, and with obvious relief.

'And I'd better go back and join my father for breakfast,' said David. 'Not that I'm hungry, but he'll wonder where I am.'

'I'll stay on and collect the bill,' said Mr Westwood. 'When mine host returns. He seems to have gone for a walk.'

Following the other two out into the street David saw a brief scene which he didn't immediately understand. The café-owner, with a sour smile on his face, was crossing the road back towards the café and, on the opposite pavement, Tim's father, clutching a lunch-tin and presumably on the way to the mill, was shouting after Tim and Jane, who were walking away from him towards the centre of the town and school.

'You were seen,' he was shouting.

'We weren't trying not to be,' Tim called back, without turning or slowing down.

'I'm warning you,' yelled his father. 'I'll go to the police. They'll have him for drugs. I'm warning you.'

Tim and Jane walked on without looking back. Mr Thornby turned and continued his walk to work. He saw David, still standing outside the café, but he didn't acknowledge him.

The café-owner went into his café to collect Mr Westwood's money.

EIGHT

Late in the day, when the volunteers had finished scratching carefully in the earth and had gone to eat, David stood on the site with his father. They looked without speaking at what had been done. Disregarding the quietly misting rain, the team had worked doggedly on and by now quite a large portion of the mosaic was clear. It didn't make much sense to David. Someone had been enthusiastic about the decorative border but the main subject of the picture lay under varying depths of earth and, accordingly, had been cleared patchily.

'Is it good?' he said at last.

'In even better condition than I predicted,' said the Professor. He looked at David and then back at the ground again. 'Do anything for you?' he asked, with a slightly odd expression on his face.

'Should it?' said David. 'I'll let you know when I see more of it.'

'Yes. Well I don't need to see more of it to be able to state quite categorically that it does depict Diana.'

'Honestly? Which way up?'

'She's facing us. The crescent moon on her forehead was cleared this afternoon.' He pointed.

'I see it,' said David. 'I wasn't looking at it properly. It really is Diana?'

'It really is Diana.'

'Then Mr Westwood was right?'

'Then Mr Westwood was right.'

They both laughed.

'He's incredible,' said David. 'Are you impressed?'

'He was right – and I shall tell him so if he comes along. Look here, I don't particularly like doing this but I have to have a talk with you about him.'

'What do you mean?'

'A Mr Thornby has been down to see me.'

'Tim's father.'

'Yes. Apparently you and his two chat with Mr Westwood sometimes.'

'Yes, we do.'

'This Mr Thornby isn't keen on the association. He thinks it's unhealthy for a man of Westwood's age to befriend three youngsters – a point on which I don't agree – but he also thinks Westwood takes drugs, which he may very well do. I suspected it myself, as a matter of fact. Thornby thinks he's a bad influence and he also thinks you're responsible for his two getting involved. He wants me to warn you off Westwood, so I'm warning you.'

'I see.'

'You know very well I don't generally interfere with your arrangements. But if he is involved with drugs, then Thornby's got a genuine worry.'

'What if he is? Do you think I'm going to ask for a free handout?'

'I think it very unlikely. But I don't know anything

about these other two and apparently you're their leader.'

'Their leader! I'd like to see me lead Tim somewhere he didn't want to go. Are you telling me not to talk to Mr Westwood?'

'What you do is your business, and mine. But leave the other two out of it.'

David shrugged. 'OK,' he said.

'Is Westwood's friendship very important to you?' asked his father.

'Yes it is. He's one of the most interesting people I've ever met. His approach to archaeology is totally different . . .'

'Oh yes, I *am* aware of that!'

'He's just so interesting. He makes you think about things in a different way.' David decided to try out Mr Westwood's view of consciousness on his father. 'He's made me see,' he explained, 'that there is as much consciousness in the space between here and here,' tapping his own forehead and his father's shoulder, 'as there is inside my skull.'

'That may very well be true,' said his father drily. 'But I don't think it's anything to boast about.'

'Oh look – you must have some respect for him now – now that the mosaic – *your* mosaic – is as he said?'

Professor Birch walked slowly along one of the catwalks away from David, and as slowly back again, his hands in the back pockets of his trousers and his head bent, although he was no longer looking at the Roman artwork at his feet.

'He's chasing a chimera,' he said at last. 'I've come across them before, these people. The world of what you might call alternative archaeology is full of them. They give up everything of real value in their lives to pursue something they believe to be external. In fact it's all inside their own heads and they'll never catch up with it, any more than anyone is ever going to get to the end of a rainbow.'

'Or it could be,' said David, 'that he's being true to himself. He's given up all the things society thinks are important. That can't have been easy at his age – with people like you looking superior about it.'

'I see a pathetic, middle-aged man who has abandoned wife and job and put his whole future at risk to try and get back to his youth. If you see an intellectual revolutionary with the courage to be true to his ideals then I can't stop you admiring him. But don't get entangled – if you get caught up in any kind of drug scene, you're a fool.'

'Unlike you and Mr Thornby, I'm not obsessed with drugs.'

'Good.'

'Apart from anything else, he's interested in the Weeping Stones and he knows a tremendous amount. When I think of him, and then I think of that pompous Mr Thatcher . . .'

His father laughed. 'Ah, well, Thatcher . . .' he said.

'Don't you think he's pompous?'

'He's the kind of man who unerringly chooses the unimportant in his surroundings and latches on to that. There's quite a nice little rustic shrine under the motorway here, and that surprisingly well-preserved circle on the moors, but his attention is held by the possibility of tracing a very, very minor road – barely more than a driveway connecting the shrine with the nearest Roman B road.'

'I thought you didn't attach any importance to the circle?'

'I attach a lot more to the shrine – but I hardly attach any to the road.'

Something occurred to David. 'Mr Thatcher calls it a villa,' he said. 'Not a shrine.'

'Yes, he would. He knows Romans built villas. He's been told it's a shrine, and he believes it, but he can't quite make the necessary manoeuvre to get the idea lodged inside his head.'

'Have you seen his office?'

'No, thank you.'

'It's packed with rubbish. All the cupboards and drawers are half open.'

'Gaping in amazement, presumably.'

David found himself searching for some other derogatory remark to make to prolong the conversation. He realized he was actually prepared to invent some silliness that he and his father could dissect together. As his mind rummaged through its vague picture of Mr Thatcher amidst his belongings, his father said, 'Poor old Thatcher. He *is* a sincere enthusiast.'

'Yes.'

They looked at the mosaic in silence for a couple of minutes.

'Look,' said David suddenly. 'Failing Mr Westwood,

how am I supposed to find out about the circle? I really believe something's happening up there – and I think Mr Westwood knows. I know nobody else does.'

Professor Birch took out his handkerchief, sneezed, blew his nose, replaced the handkerchief and jumbled his arms about in the air. 'You'll just have to use your ingenuity,' he said.

NINE

He caught them after school. Tim came out first, and Jane caught up with him when she had shaken herself free of a crowd of giggling classmates that Tim eyed morosely but wouldn't speak to.

'I've come to fetch you,' said David excitedly, 'because I've been to the stones again and they're electric. You've got to come and see. It must have something to do with all the water that's everywhere – it's turning into a marsh up there.'

'You serious?' said Tim.

'Yes, really. Come on. It won't take long.'

'I feel sick,' said Jane.

'Oh, save us!' said Tim. 'There's always something.'

'I do. I have all day.'

'You'd better go home then. Tell them I'll not be long.'

'But I want to come to the circle.'

'Come then.'

'You said to go home.'

'You are a trial, aren't you?' said Tim.

'You don't want me to come with you. I can tell.'

'Of course you can come. I can hardly stop you, can I? Unless I tie you to a tree or something.'

'You must come, Jane,' said David. 'You were the first one who felt anything up there.'

'It's no good trying to get on the right side of her,' said Tim. 'She's in a silly mood.'

Jane said, quite quietly, 'if you really wanted me to come with you, I'd be in a nice mood.'

'If you were in a nice mood we'd really want you to come with us,' said Tim. 'Beat that,' and he turned and walked towards the bridge.

The slope of the moors was even wetter and slipperier than before. They all made heavy weather of climbing it. Jane seemed to get entirely stuck at one point and held up her hands like a child. 'Help me,' she said.

'What *is* the matter with you?' demanded Tim. 'You can climb as well as I can.'

David went back a few paces and began to haul Jane upwards.

'I'm churning,' she explained.

'What!' said Tim from ahead.

'My tummy's churning – like when you're going to a party.'

'I thought you felt sick?'

'The churning makes me feel sick.'

They moved on up, the waterlogged earth closing around their shoes and trying to suck them off their feet.

'Yesterday you were on about toothache,' said Tim.

'I've still got it.'

'Oh blimey!'

'Well I haven't got it to annoy you. I don't like it either.'

'Why do you have to get everything that's going?'

'It isn't just me. A lot of people have got toothache – that's why I can't go till Saturday.'

'And two days ago you had peas in your neck. It never stops.'

'I've *still* got peas in my neck,' roared Jane, and she snatched free of David and stood quite still, except that her feet slid a little way back down the slope of their own accord. '*And* toothache. *And* churning. And *some* people would be sympathetic.' And she burst into noisy tears.

Tim floundered back down to her and drummed awkwardly on her back with one hand. 'Think about something else,' he said. 'Don't go all feeble on me. You've always been all right before.'

'I'm not all right now. I hate it.'

'Hate what?'

'Everything. It's all inside me and vibrating and full of crying and I *hate* it.' She snuffled angrily into her handkerchief.

'Come on,' said David, embarrassed. 'Let's get up there and on to level ground – then we can talk.'

Jane pulled away from offers of help and scrambled perfectly competently to the top of the ridge – where there waited a pale, rainwashed sky, stones that were darkly wet, and John Westwood, standing very still between the two tallest.

David caught at Tim's arm. 'I didn't know he was here,' he whispered. 'Your father . . .'

Tim shook away his hand. 'Can't be helped now,' he said.

There was a strange pause. Jane stood and stared at Mr Westwood, her eyes screwed up and still ready to cry. Mr Westwood's eyes were closed, his hands making contact with the stone on each side of him. Tim and David had stopped some paces behind Jane.

For a few seconds there was complete silence, except for a faint and strange humming noise that David, for one terrible moment, thought was coming from the stones themselves. In that moment he saw them as a circle of men who had indeed been turned to stone, as the old stories said, and who, as they hummed their wordless chant, were preparing to become men once more.

And then he saw Tim glance towards the cleft and away again and he realized that Tim had heard it, too, and that Tim had understood what it really was – nothing more sinister than the sound of the textile mill in action, a sound magnified by the deep and hollow cleft.

Mr Westwood opened his eyes and let his hands drop back to his sides.

'The current has gone for the moment,' he said. 'It waxes and wanes like the tides. Each time it is stronger.'

David was struck sharply by a strange thought. The knowledge, the extraordinary knowledge that Mr Westwood devoured so insatiably – was that the true meaning of the 'fairy food'? By seeking and tasting the knowledge had he bound himself to something not of this world?

Tim walked quickly forwards and placed the flat of his hand on the top of the stone nearest to him – a short, crooked stone that leant over to one side. He turned and looked at David and shrugged. 'Nothing at all,' he said.

'Ah, you brought the unbeliever up to feel the current for himself,' said Mr Westwood. 'You should have come five minutes earlier or three hours later.' He seemed unperturbed.

'What causes it?' said David.

Mr Westwood spread his hands. 'They're active,' he said.

'Stones can't give off electricity,' said Tim.

'These ones do,' said Mr Westwood simply. He backed out of the circle. 'But not now. Not at the moment.' He moved round to where Jane stood, rather alone. 'You shouldn't really be here,' he said, quite quietly.

Jane's face, which had been poised on the brink of despair, crumpled up completely. '*Why* shouldn't I?' and she was crying again.

Mr Westwood moved closer and took hold of her arm, just above the elbow. 'It doesn't make you happy to be here,' he said. 'It doesn't give you peace. It's all inside you now.' He placed his other hand on her other elbow and then snatched both hands sharply away.

Jane looked startled. 'What was that?' she said.

Mr Westwood smiled at her. 'I got an electric shock from you,' he said.

'I felt it!' said Jane.

'Why!' David demanded sharply.

'Their time is close,' said Mr Westwood. 'They are calling very loudly. Calling to all that they own. Calling to white things, to the things of the moon – female things, water, all liquid, all people under the sway of the moon, all Cancerian people, like Jane. See how the moon's plants are growing in the centre. See how rich the trefoil is. Everyone in the valley is beginning to feel it, but the women feel it most strongly. When is your birthday, Jane?'

'On the eighth.'

'It would be better if you went away for a while,' said Mr Westwood.

'How can she go away?' said Tim. He walked over to Jane and put his arm across her shoulders. 'She isn't electric,' he said. 'She's perfectly all right.'

'She's better at the moment,' agreed Mr Westwood. 'I drew it out of her.'

Jane turned to Tim. 'I do feel better,' she said, and she did seem calmer.

'You see, you are a Cancerian,' said Mr Westwood. 'You are under the sway of the circle.'

Tim was looking hard at Mr Westwood. 'She has seemed different lately,' he said.

'All the negative, watery elements in you are being brought to the fore,' Mr Westwood went on, talking only to Jane. 'These things are always in you, but as the circle calls them forth they become more difficult to control. To be at peace one must achieve balance and harmony. This is never easy, but for you at the moment it is almost impossible. The stones' power is accenting one aspect only. They are vibrating on a very low note which creates unease in everyone – but which is far more noticeable to you and to people like you.'

Jane put her hands to her neck. 'My glands are all swollen,' she said.

'I'm not at all surprised.'

'And I churn – inside.'

'I know.'

'When is all this supposed to stop?' said Tim.

'It will reach a climax,' said Mr Westwood.

'And what happens to her then?' said Tim.

'I don't know,' said Mr Westwood. He looked at Jane again. 'You will be all right,' he said. 'There is a dark side to the moon, but there is a light side, too. It will be very hard, but you can control what's happening in you.'

'So it's up to me?' said Jane, watching him intently.

'It's always up to you,' said Mr Westwood.

'But the circle,' said Jane. 'What am I supposed to do about that?'

'Oh, the responsibility for that is not on you,' said Mr Westwood. 'That is on everyone. As soon as I understand I will tell you. We will all stop it together.'

'So it's definitely something bad that's happening,' said David, 'if it must be stopped?'

Mr Westwood gazed at him for a moment. 'It is something which is out of control,' he said. 'It can be brought under control, but it must first be understood.'

'How can we understand it?' said David.

'I am working as hard as I can,' said Mr Westwood. 'Believe me. Everything I have ever studied has led me towards this. But I had thought I was studying things which were out of use. I hadn't realized that there was this urgency. I had thought their time was long past, but that one day I would test my theories by deliberately reactivating them in a controlled experiment. I was not prepared to find one of them already active.'

'Is it something you've done?' said David.

'I don't think so. I really don't think so. I must go back now. I must continue to work. I will understand very soon and then I will tell you.' He turned back to Jane. 'It would be better if you could go away,' he said again. 'More comfortable. But you can be all right. At worst it will pass through you like a storm. But there is peace on the other side.'

He made as if to start down the slope. 'Oh wait!' called David. 'Have you been to the dig?'

Mr Westwood paused and turned to look at him.

'You were right about the mosaic. It is Diana.'

Mr Westwood nodded. 'Yes, I know. I knew.'

'But it's a Roman mosaic.'

'Yes.'

'Then the Romans thought the area belonged to the moon, too?'

'Oh – they knew it.'

David was surprised. Despite their complex mythology he had somehow always regarded the Romans as a purely practical people, concerned with baths and roads and other forms of engineering. He had thought that must be why they appealed to his father.

'Does it help?' he said.

Mr Westwood spread his hands. 'It's all part of it,' he said. 'But then I knew it already.' And he turned and began down the slope once more.

'Wait!' said David again. 'There's something I have to know.'

Mr Westwood turned and waited. 'Well?' he said.

'About drugs,' said David. 'They– they say you take drugs.'

TEN

Mr Westwood walked the few steps back to them with such a sense of purpose that David, who was nearest to him, took one step away – but he halted well short of them.

'Now listen to me,' he said. 'Listen, because this matters. I began to use certain mind-altering drugs about five years ago in the hope of finding a short cut to the knowledge I was looking for.

'I met strange and magical things, but the only knowledge I found was this – that illusion blurs the perceptions even while seeming to heighten them. If you wish to arouse phantoms, then do so, but know that they are only phantoms. If you wish to look at the world through a coloured filter then do so, but don't argue with a man who sees the world through his own eyes . . .

'We know little enough about perception. We know that our five or six senses are very limited but we don't know how limited. So how can we presume to interfere? If you knew nothing about televisions would you even consider opening up the back of one to tinker about in the hope of improving reception?

'It is perfectly possible to sharpen one's own awareness without cheating by using chemicals. And if you try to come on the truth by a cheating method you will only be offered a distortion of the truth – truth will cheat you in return.'

He stopped – suddenly looking very, very tired indeed.

'I try to approach the truth as it should be approached,' he said. 'But now the drugs I used are using me. They have left my mind just a little clouded – my thinking just a little woollier than it might once have been. And now I can't choose when I take them. There are times when I shake and need their help. Does that answer you?'

David was trying to hold on to the drift of what had been said. 'Yes,' was all he could offer.

Jane was looking at the Weeping Stones, standing with her shoulders rounded and her toes turned slightly inwards, in a self-protective attitude. Tim was staring stolidly at Mr Westwood and whatever was going on inside his head left no mark on his features.

'Who told you?' said Mr Westwood.

'My father – and his father,' said David. 'But they were only guessing.'

'I hadn't realized it was so obvious.'

'I'm sorry,' said David awkwardly.

'I am not offended. I will do anything to prevent any one of you from embarking on my foolishness.'

He looked tired and tatty – and almost more lonely than David could bear. He wanted to say, 'You're our friend – we like you,' but it seemed so conceited to assume that their – his – friendship would be of value to Mr Westwood that he said nothing. It occurred to him that he wanted to cry for the first time in years, but he wasn't very sure why.

Mr Westwood seemed to wait a moment – for something to happen or something to be said – but nothing did happen and no one spoke, so he turned away for the third time and made his way down the slope towards the town. Half-way he raised his hand in a kind of salute, but he didn't look back.

He left them in an unreal world, enclosed in the poor visibility that damp air brings. David felt almost as if they were part of a tableau, locked in a misty crystal ball with the standing stones. He wandered over to the nearest one and touched it, but it was as Mr Westwood had said, the current no longer flowed.

'I did want you to feel the electric current,' he said to Tim as they began to descend.

Tim didn't answer. Jane still walked with her shoulders curved forwards. It was as if she was trying to shut out the circle and its influence but, in order to do so, had to shut out everyone else as well.

As they neared level ground once more, they could see Mr Thornby standing on the bridge, apparently waiting for them. He walked to meet them and as he drew nearer David could see that his face was distorted with anger. With sinking heart he realized that Mr Westwood must have passed this way minutes earlier and conclusions would not be hard to draw.

'I saw you,' said Mr Thornby, when they were still some distance apart. 'I was on my way back from work and I saw you go up there. I went home and watched you through my binoculars. You've got some nerve. How many times have you been warned?'

'We didn't know he was there when we went up,' said Tim, apparently intending to walk on over the bridge.

His father blocked his way. 'Then you should have come straight down. I watched. I saw him pawing her.'

There was a total silence for a perceptible moment while the rushing of the swollen river filled the air.

Then, 'You've got a very nasty mind,' said Tim.

'What am I for, if not to look out for both of you,' said his father. 'I'm not vindictive. If you'd kept your distance like you were told I'd not have said anything. Now I'm going to the police. They're tough on drugs these days.'

'There's no need,' began David. 'He was telling us . . . up there . . . that we should never . . .'

Mr Thornby cut in. 'It was your idea to go up there and meet him, I don't doubt,' he said. 'You've got a lot to answer for. But your own Dad can talk to you – you're not my problem.'

Jane walked to the parapet of the bridge, leaned her elbows on it, cupped her hands around her face and wept quietly.

'He was trying to put us *off*,' said David, shaken by the very real anger in front of him and unable to say as much as he wanted to.

Without another word Mr Thornby turned and walked away from them, not in the direction of the mill but back towards the town and, presumably, the police station.

David looked to Tim. 'Can't we make him understand?' he almost begged.

'It's never been done,' said Tim.

'But it's so unfair – after what Mr Westwood said. And it's all our fault.'

Tim shrugged.

'Your mother – if we explained to her – could she talk to him?'

'She leaves that kind of thing up to him. She'd not interfere.'

'Don't you care?'

Tim looked across to Jane, where she leant over the parapet of the bridge.

'Look,' he said, quietly and fiercely to David, 'you've got to stop playing this daft game about that crumbling old relic up there.'

'It isn't a game!'

'She's getting badly spooked by it – can't you see that?'

'I see, but I don't think that ignoring what's happening is going to help her.'

'Do you know what's happening? Does that daft old modern-day wizard know what's happening?'

'No.'

'Well then!'

'Well then! I know *something* is – don't you?'

Tim shrugged.

'*Don't* you?'

Tim didn't say anything. He looked across at Jane again.

'Well give me *some* kind of answer,' said David.

'All right,' said Tim. 'I'm trying to keep myself free of the air of magic and mystery you two surround yourselves with. At one time I thought it was silly but harmless. She may be a pain sometimes, but she is my sister, remember, and I don't like to see her put into this kind of state. You and Mr Westwood – you make it sound as if someone's going to come in the night and drag her up there and sacrifice her to the moon or something. And she's quite capable of believing something like that if it's told to her often enough – so just lay off. Will that do for an answer?'

'You never *get* anywhere with people,' said David. 'I thought you were listening to him up there and taking it all in. You even said yourself that Jane's been different lately – *before* she was told a thing about the moon and her being Cancer and all that. Now you're right back to pretending nothing's strange.'

Tim crossed to Jane. 'Come on home for tea,' he said. 'The river's full enough without you crying into it.'

'At least I can go and warn Mr Westwood,' David said to their retreating backs. But if he hoped they would offer to come too, he was disappointed.

He lingered on the bridge for a while, watching the earth-cloudy water as it swept out of sight below him. Two empty Coke cans were caught against the base of the bridge. The water jostled them together and their complaining rattle irritated him even more than their presence. He was fairly sure that if he climbed down the bank he could retrieve them without getting his feet wet, but before he had a chance to try, the river flicked them free of the stonework and carried them under the bridge and out of his sight.

He thought that once upon a time men had probably

brought gifts to this river. In gratitude for its life-giving presence they would have offered some kind of sacrifice – or at the very least there would have been an annual ritual to placate and honour its spirit. Now – although it was just as important to their livelihood as ever it had been – all they had to offer it was rubbish, waste, things they didn't want, which clogged its beds and damaged its wildlife and caught in the lowest branches of the trees that bent over its banks. They might talk a lot about love but they definitely didn't know how to love a river.

And yet this river – with its two Coke cans, its dye and its wool grease – was clean, as rivers go.

Leaning over the parapet on his elbows and forearms, rocking himself to and fro and half lifting his feet from the ground, he tried to decide just how he should word his warning to Mr Westwood. He knew quite well that he was deliberately postponing the confrontation. How could he tell Mr Westwood that Mr Thornby didn't consider him fit company for his children?

He still had no particular speech in mind when he turned from the river and made for the bed and breakfast house, remembering that Mr Westwood had said he was going back to work.

When he went in at the front door he almost bumped into Mrs Foster who was in the hall, apparently standing and staring into space because she didn't appear to be doing anything.

'Is Mr Westwood in his room?' David asked.

'No,' said Mrs Foster. 'You've just missed him.'

'What – he's gone out again? Do you know where?'

Mrs Foster gazed at him. 'The police came and took him not a minute since,' she said.

ELEVEN

David went upstairs and shut himself into his room until his mind should stop rocking.

He sat on the edge of the bed. A silly chant travelled through his head . . . 'They're coming to take me away, boom boom, they're coming to take me away.' And they actually had. Threats can be so empty – and the threat to the very presence of a solid, adult person had seemed emptier than most. But he was gone, wholly gone. And the river ran ever higher and the centre of the circle was now a marshy mess and the grim stones threatened.

'They're coming to take me away.'

It wasn't so much going through his head as running round inside it, wearing a groove.

'They're coming to take me away.'

It wasn't even relevant – no one was coming to take him away. He wondered if Mr Westwood had thought of the song when the police car had arrived. He lay back on the bed and stretched out, with his shoes on. He tilted his head and looked down at his feet which were, he knew perfectly well, making marks on the duvet.

The only person capable of talking sense about what was happening was now out of reach. What was left to do?

Lying there, inert and without any energy, he began to

wonder why he felt as he did about Mr Westwood. Why he was so sure that Mr Westwood was right? It seemed like treachery, but he felt too dispirited to try and check the train of thought.

In his head, in his memory, he could see two possible Westwoods. One of them the man he had first thought him to be, with the guts to pursue what he saw to be important despite all opposition. But equally it was very obvious that he was dabbling with strong forces. What was there to say that he was strong enough, wise enough, to do this? Might it not be that he had indeed eaten the food of the fairies and, if so, was he a person to trust?

The idea of the fairy food was lodged the more firmly in David's mind because he didn't understand it. But if there was a truth that lay behind fairy stories, there must also be a truth that lay behind pomegranate seeds and honey cakes. And if he accepted that the Romans understood the area and had dedicated their shrine to Diana because of it, then he might as well accept that Persephone's visit to the underworld had meaning – and was reflected in every story and poem which dealt with fairies as powerful forces, rather than as impotent, doll-like creatures who dished out wishes in threes, like party hats.

In every story it is made plain that eating the fairy food is an irrevocable move, and that those who once taste it pursue it to the detriment of their lives, right to their lives' end. It is never a beneficial or a nourishing food; it is a teasing food, and it changes the personality.

His mind began to work very fast. He thought of

fairy stories – which made him think of fairy rings – of toadstools – of mushrooms. And from mushrooms come drugs, hallucinogenic drugs.

And that – all the time – was the fairy food – the food that no human could sample if he wanted to retain his freedom. Little wonder that Mr Westwood hadn't commented when he had brought up the subject before. So did the fact that Mr Westwood had made that mistake invalidate all his ideas?

Whatever the answer to that, it was clear that Mr Westwood was – had been – the only person to concern himself with the activities of the circle in what seemed like a rational manner. And he had gone to an unspecified destination, taking with him all that he had discovered.

Unless he had left notes in his room.

A conventional upbringing had not really fitted David to break into someone's room and go through his belongings. He conducted a very long dialogue within himself before he even got up from his bed. His main anxiety was not so much that he might be found and asked what he was doing, but that Mr Westwood himself might not approve. If he could only receive Mr Westwood's permission to go through his papers he wouldn't mind what his father, or Mrs Foster, or the police, might say. But if he had been in a position to ask, the trespass wouldn't have been necessary, so that was a pointless thought.

He had to go and look because then at least he would have tried to do something. Better a positive action which was wrong than a negative action which was wrong – he thought. Ridiculous to allow social convention to get in the way in such a dramatic situation.

He began badly, by creeping cautiously out of his own room. He realized that there was no reason on earth why he should not be walking out of his bedroom door and down the stairs, and that no one who saw him would challenge him. He reached Mr Westwood's door, one landing down, and tried the handle, although he had by now become certain that he would have to go outside and try to climb in at the window. To his great surprise, the door opened easily enough and he slipped inside and closed it behind him.

No one was likely to look for him, and if he made no noise he saw no reason why he should be disturbed. But it was then, inside the room and leaning on the door, that he realized that it was more than just social convention which had held him back. Mr Westwood's room had not been searched because he had told the police where to look. It was like the room of a man who had stepped out for half an hour. The books, the papers, the pencils strewn on the table under the window were strewn in an intensely personal way – many of the books had strips of paper hanging out from between their pages and the papers, though untidy, were grouped. This was the temporary desk of a man quietly pursuing his own researches and to sit at it, to riffle through the papers, would be a very serious intrusion.

For a long time David leant against the door and looked across the room and the table and out of the window beyond – because there he saw the trees of Mrs

Foster's back garden and the back of another house, and it was all right to look at those.

It was sad, he thought, that Mr Westwood should have been given a room at the back of the house where he couldn't look out on the circle – but nevertheless this was where he had sat while he studied and tried to unravel the meaning of the Weeping Stones.

Then David remembered something that had happened to him a long time ago. Once, while walking along the road to school, he had had a very good idea. Something had distracted him and the idea had left his head before it had had time to take root. For the rest of the day he had not even been able to remember the flavour of it, or the subject it had been concerned with. Then, that same evening, on the way home from school, the idea had dropped back into his head again at exactly the place where it had left him. He had felt at the time as if it had hung in the air all day, waiting for him to pass underneath again. He wondered if any of Mr Westwood's ideas were hanging in the air above his chair and, holding firmly on to that thought, he moved over to the chair and sat down in it.

And inevitably he looked at the table in front of him. Gradually, book titles made sense to him. He saw works on all the subjects Mr Westwood had said were essential – he saw maps, some of them hand-drawn – he saw a book of tables setting out the movements of the planets for the past many years, and he saw some sheets of paper bearing the most intricate geometrical and mathematical calculations he had ever come across. He stared at these unembarrassed because their meaning was so far from him that he could not possibly spy on the thoughts that had prompted them. And right in front of him, half covering a diagram of the stone circle, he saw quite a small spiral-bound notebook – fat, and with a nice design on the outside. After a moment he picked it up and flipped through it very fast. There was writing on four different pages – but not consecutive pages. It was as if Mr Westwood had seized the book and written down ideas as they came to him, at random.

Since these notes would be as incomprehensible to him as the diagrams and calculations, David reasoned, glancing through them could hardly matter. But they were not incomprehensible. They were written as Mr Westwood might speak. They were the simple straightforward conclusions that had been reached by way of long hours of study and calculation.

The first note was written on the first page.

The zodiac contains three water signs. There is Pisces in the late spring when the movement of the water is underground. In the autumn there is Scorpio, governing the natural time of death when fluid is taken away, leaves dry and fall, sap drops back into the plants. And in high summer there is Cancer, ruled by the moon, mover of the tides.

His slow and formal approach to reading another person's private writings was now concluded. David leaned back in the chair and quietly turned the two or three pages to the next entry.

The legends have been corrupted. It is not that the stones weep for their sins – as some seventeenth-century puritan chose to say – but that they weep spring water to fill the drought-dried river. It is not that the stones go down to the river to drink, but that the stones give water to the thirsty river. The circle is a very fine machine to avert drought. The stones, broken down and worn as they are, are still capable of being activated when the planets are in a particular formation on five days of each year, the potential being at its height on the central day of those five, waxing before and waning after. At this time the circle has the power to draw the waters out of the earth – to conjure water from a spring deep within itself which floods down the cleft to fill the river. The very depth of the water-cut cleft is an indication that the circle was used many, many times in its day.'

David read the words twice and then turned to the third entry in the book.

Once in every generation, in this particular area, there comes a time of maximum drought and a time of maximum fluidity. The circle is geared to the sun in the middle decan of Cancer, which falls in early July – a crucial time for a drought-stricken area. It would have been activated, when the old knowledge was still alive, at the time of maximum drought, to alleviate the problem. It is now being activated not only at a point of maximum fluidity, but when the full moon is in conjunction with the sun in the middle decan of Cancer. This means that the circle has been activated at maximum power at a time when water is already available in abundance.

According to my calculations, the serious effects will begin to be felt around July 6th and will build steadily. The maximum conjunction of the sun and the full moon in this middle decan of Cancer takes place at 7 p.m. on Saturday July 8th. The effects will manifest at their peak on earth at 11 p.m. on that day.

At the least there promise to be serious floods whose effects will be felt far beyond this one valley – at worst, a build-up of water behind the immense heaps of earth created by work on the motorway bridge could bring disaster to the houses on the river side of the town. Records of the town go back eight hundred years and it appears that in all that time the circle has never been active as it is now. It is vital to discover what has activated it.

The final note came as even more of a shock. It was headed 'David' and it was a brief list of book titles. David closed the book on it, not wanting to read the list until he was given it properly.

He sank back in the chair and gazed out of the window, though he no longer saw the trees. So much for Tim saying that the legends bore as much relation to the purpose of the circle as if David himself had made up a fairy story about how and why York Minster was built, he thought. Mr Westwood had clearly been right on the edge of discovering the whole truth – perhaps actually had discovered it but hadn't had time to write down the last bit.

Everything made sense except the one thing. Obviously the circle had been designed to be used when necessary – to be 'switched on' perhaps no more than once every ten years, and then only until the object had been achieved and the river filled. Now – after maybe three thousand years of inactivity – it had somehow been turned on – and left on. But how?

The thought about York Minster had stirred something in David's mind which he tried to suppress in order to pursue the more vital subject of the circle — but the stirrings were so insistent that he decided to get them out of the way first. So he let himself remember the time he and his father had visited the Minster very early one morning, had looked at the empty stateliness inside and been impressed. But his father, who was not a religious man, had nevertheless said that they should really have come to a service because the great church was incomplete without music to give it life.

Could it be sound that activated the circle? Vibrations that brought it to life? If so — what sound? In its day it would presumably have been chanting — the chanting of men's voices. But now?

David thought of all the times he had stood near the circle. In his mind he saw the stones, ancient and worn but still imposing, still awe-inspiring. He felt the soft misting rain on his face. He heard the light wind, the occasional distant buzz of traffic from the town — and something else. A faint, strange humming noise. He'd noticed it up there more than once, but he remembered that particular time when he and Jane and Tim had climbed to the top of the ridge and found Mr Westwood, a hand on each of the tallest stones, eyes closed, apparently communing with the circle. That time the humming had been very noticeable and for one awful moment David had thought the stones themselves were chanting. Then Tim had looked over at the deep cleft in the rock and he had understood that it was only the sound of the textile mill, way down below, at the lowest point of the chasm. The textile mill — chanting.

He leaned forward, staring unseeing out of the window. Why had the mill never created this effect before? The new plant! Tim's father had said there was new plant in the mill, which was why they could meet the latest big order – if they worked overtime.

By pure chance, then, the new plant in the textile mill was exactly reproducing a sound which had not been heard on these moors for thousands of years. A sound which was amplified by the deep cleft which cut through the hillside, from behind the mill almost to the circle. A sound which, now the mill was working round the clock, hummed on relentlessly, day and night, in that unusually wet summer, as the rain fell and the river waters rose – and the circle responded to the mill's song and poured forth its spring.

TWELVE

Professor Birch listened throughout the evening meal to David's new understanding of the situation – or, at least, he ate in silence while David talked.

'It makes a nice story,' he said, when it was over.

David glanced at his watch. 'Well – what am I going to do?'

His father drank from his post-dinner mug of tea. 'You tell me,' he said.

'You *were* listening?'

'Yes.'

'I'll have to stop the mill, won't I?'

'I don't think you'll find that very easy.'

'Either it'll have to be stopped or else they'll have to go back to whatever they used to do – before they had this new plant and generator.'

'Ah. It's only the new plant you're bothered about?'

'Well yes,' said David. 'This has never happened before, so obviously the old plant didn't strike the same note as the new plant. You *weren't* listening!'

There was a brief pause. The two elderly budgerigars fidgeted in their cage.

'I'm not absolutely sure how serious you are about all this, or what you want me to do,' said his father at last.

'I just don't know how to go about stopping the mill

– or who to tell. Do I go to the town council – or what? I thought you'd know.'

'It makes a nice story,' his father repeated, 'but I don't think you should carry it too far.'

'You don't believe it!'

'You said that Mr Westwood himself admitted he'd drummed up phantoms – you know what he was telling you, I take it?'

'I suppose he was saying he gave himself hallucinations.'

'I would think so.'

'Yes, but this wasn't one of them. He as good as said he knew how to study this without getting caught up in hallucinations.'

'I expect he would be the first to admit that his judgment isn't as sound as it once was.'

'But the idea the *mill* is activating the stones is mine, not his, and I'm not hallucinating,' said David. 'Twice I've felt the electricity in the stones myself. Twice!'

'If there's some freak effect up there it may be worth investigating. But if you want to arouse serious interest it's best to stop at what you know. Twice, the stones seemed to you to be charged with electricity. That's one thing. Start talking about chanting voices and apocalyptic floods and you immediately lose credibility.'

'All right,' said David. 'You're only interested in the Roman mosaic. Don't you know that floods could wash all the earth from the motorway approaches right over the dig and bury it all again – and probably break it up, too?'

'I'm very aware of that. In fact there are plans to get

all that earth shifted somewhere safer.'

'How soon?'

'Next week, I hope.'

'That won't be soon enough.'

'I don't deny the possibility of the river breaking its banks – but I greatly doubt that the stones on the moor have any connection with that possibility.'

'Look, do you want to know why I was late for this meal?'

'I never ask things like that.'

'As soon as I'd finished reading those notes – and realized – I went straight up on to the moor again. I looked down that cleft which before was just very damp and full of ferns, and now there's an actual stream in there. It comes out from the rock at the top of the cleft – really close to the circle. There isn't very much water in it yet, but it's going to build up. It's already made an enormous puddle – more like a baby lake, really – at the bottom of the cleft, and I'd guess that in a couple of hours, or less, that water will have crossed the road and met up with the river.'

'Very probably.'

'Well then?'

'It's been an exceptionally wet summer. It's rained for days and nights and even when it isn't raining the air is so damp that there's virtually no evaporation. The cleft forms a natural drainage channel for the soggy moors up there. A lot of rivers are over-full this year – not just this one. And I take it you're not blaming the circle for the rain?'

'Absolutely not. I explained. The circle was designed

to be used in time of drought. Now it's being used at a time of freak flood conditions. Possibly the river would have overflowed a bit anyway – but unless the mill is stopped the flooding is going to be a thousand times more serious.'

'How many times more serious?'

David reddened. 'Well, I don't know how many times more serious,' he said. 'Perhaps only twice as serious. Isn't it enough to know that with the circle active as it is now there's going to be even more water about at a time when there's already too much?'

'You still haven't said anything to convince me that the circle is in any way connected with the imminent flooding.'

'That's only because you're hearing it from me – second-hand. If you could have seen his notes – his calculations. If you'd been up on the moors yourself . . .'

'I don't think you're going to convince me,' said his father. 'I'm trying not to be too uncharitable, but you know perfectly well these occult archaeologists give me a pain.'

'Just because he doesn't work the way you work . . .'

'The best way to approach an archaeological problem – or any other – is to take the work of earlier specialists in the field and build on it – not throw everything out of the window and advance by way of astrology.'

'What if the earlier specialists are wrong?'

'I find it hard to be sympathetic towards people who have no respect for researchers in their own field.'

'You have no respect for him!'

'He isn't a researcher – he's a dabbler. I've talked to him, too, you know. "This whole area belongs to the moon." There's no reasoning with people who want to put a mystical interpretation on everything. There's little enough left on some of these sites for an archaeologist to work on – it's vital to stick to the realities and not go flying off into make-believe.'

'You mean it's potsherds or nothing?'

'That is a slight over-simplification.'

David rearranged his arm under the table so that he could glance at his watch without being noticed. Seven minutes. He had held his father's attention in conversation for seven minutes, an all-time record. If the situation had not been so desperate he might have paused to feel pleased with himself.

'You told me yourself,' he said, 'that there is no archaeological evidence to show that Caesar made two invasions into Britain. We only know he did because we have his writings – and the writings of Tacitus. So obviously archaeology isn't enough. We need any other piece of information we can get hold of.'

'I agree with you absolutely. I simply cannot accept that Westwood had any real information to offer.'

Despite his father's folded arms and closed face, David tilted his chair forward for a final attempt.

'Look,' he said, 'you have to accept he just *could* be right. We both know that when something in a museum is labelled "ritual object" it means no one knows what it was for. But "ritual" objects, and "ritual" structures like the Weeping Stones, might have been based on what you call "occult" ideas – astrology and numerology and things. Yes? So if someone who understands these things looks at - say - a stone circle – and sees that its proportions mean something in "occult" terms, why couldn't it be that the creators of the circle used these proportions on purpose? Why shouldn't an occultist of today be able to recognize and understand the work of an occultist of the past? Just like a present-day doctor might be interested to study ancient methods of healing. An archaeologist is only somebody who digs things up and catalogues them – that doesn't mean he's the only person in the world who can make sense of them.'

Professor Birch was watching the male budgerigar, who had tidied a loose downy feather out of its wing but appeared unable to get it unstuck from its beak.

At last he said, 'Follow it up. Carry on. I won't interfere. I never do. And I'll carry on with what I'm trying to do. Isn't that best?'

'You're afraid of getting involved in case it damages your reputation,' said David, angry and disappointed. 'That's what I think.'

'Then I'll tell you what I think. I think this ageing hippie of yours has latched on to a structure which is so ancient that no one is in a position to contradict him – whatever he says – and that he has built a fantasy around it which ties in loosely with what is happening in this area anyway. He probably believes it – he's probably deceived himself. I'm sorry that he's deceived you. However, you must make your own investigations and reach your own conclusions. But don't expect me to take your extraordinary tale seriously.'

'There's absolutely no more to be said then,' said David flatly.

'It would seem not,' said his father. 'I'm going up to my room to do some work.'

'Go where you like,' said David. 'And that's the first and only time I shall ever come to you for advice.'

THIRTEEN

All the way round to Tim's house David pursued an angry dialogue with his father inside his head. Part of his annoyance was directed towards himself for not being able to go it alone – for needing the comfort and support of some other person.

He was so concerned with the problem that, unbelievably, he had almost entirely forgotten the incident on the bridge and was rather taken aback when Mr Thornby opened the door to him. He was suddenly faced with the possibility that he might not be especially welcome and in any case made rather a bad start by blurting out, 'You got your way. He's in prison.'

'Most likely he'll only get a fine,' said Mr Thornby.

'Would it be all right for me to see Tim?'

Mr Thornby opened the door wider and stood aside. 'I've nowt against you,' he said. 'I dare say you meant no harm. But you can't take risks these days.' With Mr Westwood well out of the way he seemed more relaxed.

In the front room the whole family was sitting round the television set. Though he was invited, David didn't sit down with them. 'Come for a walk?' he said to Tim, trying not to sound too urgent.

'I'm full. And there's a good film on the telly,' said Tim.

David was at a loss, but Mrs Thornby leant forward and prodded her son on the knee with a knitting needle. 'Go on, you great lump,' she said. 'You'll be getting a middle-aged spread before you've come of age the way you go.'

Tim hauled himself reluctantly upright. Jane fixed David with large eyes. David ignored her.

Outside, Tim said, 'You'll have Baby Jane all upset again. It doesn't take much to make her feel unloved.'

'Sorry,' said David. 'But you said you wanted her kept out of this circle business and I didn't think there was much chance you'd listen to me if she was around.'

'Where are we going, then?'

'Anywhere. Down to the river, if you like. I just wanted to tell you what I've found out.'

Tim was silent while they walked and David spoke, with no expression on his face to indicate whether or not he was listening – or impressed.

'So you see,' David wound up, 'it's vital the mill is closed, even if only for a week. I can't decide who to go to or where to start – I thought if you'd help me . . .'

They had reached the river bank to the left of the bridge and had stopped to view the water which was fast-flowing and right up to the brink of the verge where they stood. The wide shingle beaches where David had first seen Tim and Jane were entirely under water now, and the sheep had been moved from the flat wasteland behind them, which promised to become a lake within hours. Looking across the river it was quite possible to see that the water from the cleft was flowing steadily

97

across the road and into the river itself.

'You make me sick,' said Tim quite quietly.

David thought he must have misheard. 'What?'

'You and your fancy father who can get work anywhere, any time, raking in money for something most people would think of as a hobby. You're just out of touch with reality, you. Have you any idea how dangerous it might be to force a mill closure? Have you any idea how many mills have been closed down around here already? You take a long walk in the valleys and you'll see. Stone has been used for building and all that's left is a chimney sticking up. Well – that happens here and what's my Dad supposed to do for money?'

David sucked in a very deep breath and withdrew a little from the rushing water and Tim.

'You're being short-sighted,' he said. 'If there's serious flooding the mill'll be put out of action anyway. Look over at it – I should think there's some water on the ground floor already.'

'If there's flooding it's because of the rain. No one can stop the rain.'

'I know that – but the circle is making it all worse. Can't you understand that?'

Tim didn't answer.

'As soon as you don't agree you go quiet. You won't even argue.'

'What is there to say?'

'You're mean,' said David, out of delayed reaction to Tim's outburst. 'Mean and miserly and stingy. You won't argue, you won't discuss, you won't give of yourself at all.'

'That's my problem, not yours.'

'Have you believed anything I've said about the stones? Can't you see that it's only sensible . . .'

'You're not one to talk about "sensible",' said Tim. 'You've got no sense. You ought to have heard yourself – "I'm very interested in pollution." You can be interested in fishing or science or textiles or stamps – pollution is lives, pollution is to do with our whole future – it isn't a hobby. You think I don't take it seriously enough, but I do. I take it more seriously than you do. You're playing. You say it's "interesting". I think that's wicked. You want to think what it means – you want to think what causes it, and think on, and see how you're going to fit people to live without the things they depend on. You want to use a bit of sense before you try throwing people out of work for the sake of a stickleback – or some fairy story.'

Tim turned away and walked off down the river's edge, looking into the water and then occasionally glancing up at the sky which promised more rain within the hour.

'I'll go on back, then,' David called.

He got no reply, which didn't surprise him, and he wandered away, his head full of tangled uncomfortable ideas which he could neither dismiss nor cope with.

Who could you go to at a time like this, and what was there to say that everyone wouldn't react as his father had, or as Tim had?

He walked towards the bed-and-breakfast because it was getting late and he was tired and anyway there was nowhere else to go.

He thought that he would like to walk down the main

street, clanging a bell and shouting out the story of the danger of the stones. He thought that once upon a time the town-crier would have done just that, and that of all the people who heard him there would be bound to have been a few who believed and understood and took action.

And then it struck him that the modern equivalent of the town-crier was the local media. And that focused his scattered attention in a way that made him feel much calmer. He hurried on back, walked briskly up to his room and began to note down the main points on a sheet of paper so that he could be concise and coherent if he managed to get a hearing the next morning.

FOURTEEN

The telephone call to the Regional TV Station took a long time and used up all the points on the phone card David had bought from the café in the square. Because he was nervous, and because he had no idea who he should speak to, he told most of his story to the woman on the switchboard before she could stop him.

'You want the assignments editor,' she said, 'but his line's busy. Do you want to hold?'

'Yes,' said David, which meant several minutes of standing in the damp callbox listening to a loop-tape of 'Greensleeves' and watching as his credit-rating ticked away on the display in front of him.

By the time the assignments editor finally came on the line, David heard himself gabble out a shortened version of events that was so compressed he wasn't even sure he understood it himself.

There was a brief pause and then the editor said, 'That's a pretty incredible story you've got there.'

'I know,' said David. Although he was annoyed with himself for doing it, he heard himself add, 'I'm Professor Birch's son,' and couldn't help feeling a kind of satisfaction when a slight change in the editor's tone told him that the name meant something. 'You were a great help,' he planned to say to his father when next they met.

'I've always felt that Druid circle had possibilities,' said the editor, 'but nothing like this.'

'Oh, the circle is long pre-Druid,' said David.

'Well, whatever . . .'

'And if there is flooding . . .' said David.

'Oh there *is* flooding. Only in a small way yet, but the river's over its banks in about four places – and an old girl at the edge of town who's got a well in her garden is complaining that water's coming up it. They want to evacuate her because her kitchen's already two feet under.'

David began kicking gently at the door of the phone box, too excited to keep still. 'That'll be the effect of the circle,' he said. 'There's too much water around to be accounted for by the amount of rain we've had – and as for the well, it's probably spring-fed and the stones are calling forth that spring as well as their own one. Have you had any other reports like that today? Unusual things? More than just the river overflowing its banks?'

'As a matter of fact, yes. But they're getting more attention than they might just now because of that well-known phenomenon, the silly season.'

'What?'

'Well – you know – there never seems to be much real news in the summer.'

'But whatever season it is – they're happening, aren't they? They're real!'

'Yes, they're real enough. The old girl I mentioned – she's a bit hard to evacuate because she's got a pet goat she won't be parted from and she won't let them take the goat too because she says it's only happy in its own garden. She says it's needed two milkings instead of one for the last three days – can you make anything of that?'

'Of course,' said David, so excited that he was beginning to enjoy himself. Forgetting for the moment that he was trying to avert a disaster, he almost looked forward to the inundation that would prove him – and Mr Westwood – right. 'Liquid, you see,' he said. 'It's calling forth all liquid. Everything in this area will be affected.'

'And you put all this down to sonar waves from the mill?'

'Sonar waves? I don't know. I only know the mill hits the same note as the chant that used to activate the circle. You go up there and listen – it sounds *exactly* . . .'

'Stopping the mill won't be popular.'

'I know, but there's no alternative.'

'What does the mill-manager say?'

'I haven't talked to him.'

'No?'

'No, because I didn't think he'd listen. I thought if he and everyone else all heard about the problem at once, then it would prepare the way.'

The editor laughed. 'You mean people will believe anything they see on TV?'

For a moment David had doubts. 'Well – yes,' he said. 'But no one's being conned. This is all true.'

'All right,' said the editor. 'I'm sending a crew down to get some swollen-river shots and take a look at the goat and the well. The circle's pretty close – they can make a round trip of it. If we use it, it'll be on the early evening news – will that be in time, do you think?'

'I don't know,' said David, relieved of his fleeting anxiety, 'But it's all we can do.'

'OK,' said the editor. 'Let's go for it. Stay tuned, eh?'

FIFTEEN

David herded his father away from the volunteers. 'It's going to be on TV tonight,' he said.

Professor Birch was no happier to be button-holed by his own son than by anyone else. 'What is?' he said. 'Look, I'm busy. These people have hit a snag down here and I don't want anything to go wrong.'

David glanced down at the two or three damp figures grovelling at their feet. For him they were faceless, soundless troglodytes who got more attention than they deserved. 'About the circle,' he went on urgently. 'I called the local TV station – no one else would listen – and they're going to do a piece on it. That way I thought someone might hear who was prepared to take it seriously. It could even get on National TV, I should think.'

His father looked solemn. Then he half smiled. 'If you can con a news editor into giving air-time to your crackpot theories,' he said, 'then you've come of age. You can go from eccentricity to eccentricity. There's nothing to stop you.'

He moved back to where David had found him, crouched down, and began to discuss the best way of removing a large stone, firmly wedged in tightly-packed soil, without damaging the mosaic underneath.

David turned away and, to his surprise, saw two men

making their way down over the rubble. One of them was rather formally dressed in a suit. The other, in jeans and a sweatshirt, was carrying a large camera on his shoulder.

They paused on level ground, looked across at David and his father and then began to make their way over the catwalk towards them.

'How's it going, sir?' said The Suit, ignoring David and speaking straight to his father.

Professor Birch straightened up. 'You have just walked past a large information sheet on a board up there,' he said. 'We took a lot of care to produce it in order to save ourselves the time and trouble necessary to answer casual questions.'

'I appreciate that, sir, but we're from Four Quarters Television and I'm afraid we can't interview a notice board.'

'I don't talk to reporters.'

'I know how busy you are. I just want two minutes of your time to get your views on the Druid circle.'

'*Druid* circle?' said Professor Birch.

David moved in a little closer. 'I told the man on the phone it was pre-Druid,' he said.

'So you're David Birch,' said The Suit, looking at him without much interest. He turned back to the Professor. 'I expect you know,' he said, 'that David's more interested in the Weeping Stones than your mosaic.' He took a piece of paper out of his pocket, glanced at it and put it away again. 'I plan to record a short piece to camera on his ideas,' he went on, 'against the background of your excavation. And then I'd really appreciate it if you'd add a few well-chosen words of your own . . .'

Before Professor Birch could respond, the two men moved off a little way to choose the best place for The Suit to stand. They didn't waste much time. The cameraman gave a signal and The Suit began to speak into a hand-held microphone. 'While Professor Birch, 41, the well-known archaeologist, supervises the restoration of the impressive mosaic uncovered by workmen at the site of the new motorway bridge,' he began, standing sideways as the camera panned past him to stare briefly at the muddy dig, 'his schoolboy son, David, has set his sights on the broken-down Druid circle on the moors which he says is a powerhouse of energy, all set to destroy us.

'Apparently someone has rashly pressed the "on" switch, and the Druid circle is threatening the valley with floods – and for all we know with plagues of locusts, too.

'David points the finger at Hatherley textile mill which he says is producing sonar waves which are disturbing its neighbour, the Druid circle, and David promises that if the mill isn't stopped, all hell will break loose.

'Now, as it isn't easy to stop a mill from milling, maybe someone could come up with a set of mammoth ear plugs. Failing that, I understand it's water-wings all round.

'I'm sure we'd all like to hear what the highly-respected Professor Birch thinks of his son's ideas.'

He looked around, and then smiled eagerly as if he had just made a pleasant discovery. 'Ah,' he said, 'and here he is.' The camera followed him as he walked back towards the Professor, holding out the microphone as he went.

Professor Birch looked at him with distaste. 'What's your name?' he said sharply.

'Peter Garrett,' said The Suit.

'How old are you?'

The Suit looked a little taken aback at the ferocity with which the questions were put. 'I'm 23,' he said.

'Well, Peter Garrett, 23, you haven't done much homework on archaeology have you? I, Professor Birch, 41, can vouch for that.'

'I don't get much time on each story,' said Garrett, rather anxiously.

'Tell your troubles to your editor, age unknown, not to me.'

Garrett rallied a little. 'Professor,' he said, 'these are your son's ideas, not mine.'

'Are you telling me my son referred to the stones as a Druid circle?'

'Certain words have impact. Druid is something people understand.'

'No they don't. And by its use you are misinterpreting my son's views.'

Peter Garrett attempted once more to cross the immense gulf between the Professor and himself. 'Now come on, Professor,' he said, laughing as one man to another, 'you're surely not telling me you take David's ideas seriously.'

'My son has studied the subject,' said the Professor. 'I

have not. Would you mind leaving us now? I have a great deal to do and you're in my way.'

Peter Garrett gazed at the Professor for a moment and then shrugged.

The cameraman switched off and loped away across the muddy ground, calling over his shoulder as he went, 'Just going to get some cut-away shots.'

'We'll have to edit all that out,' said Peter Garrett in a resigned voice. 'You do know how "The Professor refused to comment" will sound, don't you?'

But Professor Birch's attention was back on the excavation.

Peter Garrett pulled a mobile phone out of his pocket and walked away, talking into it. David, watching bleakly, just heard the words, 'It's a real turkey, but we might be able to make something of it . . .' before he was out of ear-shot.

'There goes my last resort,' said David, quietly but aloud.

His father looked at him and raised his eyebrows. 'I hope you've learnt from that,' he said, 'never to talk to a reporter unless there's an "r" in the month.'

SIXTEEN

Sometimes, in the past, David had indulged in long, heroic daydreams in which he stood alone against the world and – always – was proved right in the end. But the daydreams turned out to be no good practice for reality.

He felt he would have followed anyone who led, however difficult the route, but there was no leader. He even felt he could have led if only he could win the confidence of at least one follower. But it's hard to be a leader if no one is behind you and if, in any case, you don't know what you should do.

There had been a brief report on the flooding in the local evening news – with a couple of shots of the river spreading into fields some way out of town – but no mention of the stone circle or the mill. David didn't know whether to be disappointed or relieved.

Mr Westwood's disappearance was still shrouded in mystery. On Saturday morning David made another call from the telephone box in the square, this time to the local police station. But the only information the police would give him was that Mr Westwood was not there. Professor Birch said it was probable he was being held in the county town, pending an initial hearing. So there was no help from that quarter.

The last possible course of action was to go to the mill and talk to the foreman or the manager. Although he was surprised and rather shocked at his own cowardice, David couldn't make himself go. He pictured himself speaking to a man exactly like Mr Thornby, who wouldn't even find the story funny, like the reporter from Four Quarters TV, but just silly and irritating. He knew he would probably regret, for the rest of his life, not having made one lonely heroic attempt – but at the same time he couldn't think of anything he could say that would persuade a man concerned with the future of the mill to close it down. He hoped that in later years he would be able to remember just how impossible action had been.

Saturday lunchtime came and he sat opposite his father for the meal, which passed mostly in silence. Professor Birch didn't appear to notice that David hardly ate anything. Mrs Foster asked rather anxiously if there was something wrong with the food but David said, 'I'm just not hungry,' and she didn't pursue the point.

His stomach churned and the palms of his hands were wet.

Eventually Mrs Foster brought in the customary mugs of tea. She hesitated beside the Professor and then said, 'I'm so sorry to bother you, but I wonder if you'd mind if I asked for your help?'

'Not at all. What can I do?'

'Well,' she half laughed. 'It sounds so silly. It's just that there's something wrong with both the kitchen taps. I've turned them off but . . . the water's still coming out. I suppose it must be the washers. I have tried turning the water off at the mains to check, but I can't move the tap.'

'I don't know anything about waterworks,' said Professor Birch. 'But I'll come and look.'

The front door bell rang, long and loudly.

'Oh. Excuse me,' said Mrs Foster and went out to answer it.

David, alerted, rose to go and look at the mysterious taps, but he bumped into Mr Thatcher in the doorway of the room and was jostled back inside again.

'Professor!' said Mr Thatcher. 'I've just been down to the dig. The river's right over. I've called the volunteers out – we must make a wall of sandbags or else there'll be a terrible mess. Will you come?'

'Oh, just take a look in the kitchen first,' said Mrs Foster over Mr Thatcher's shoulder.

'Give me a chance,' said the Professor, looking harassed. 'Er – yes – just a minute, Mrs Foster. Wait here, Thatcher.'

'Professor, this is really urgent,' called Mr Thatcher as the Professor followed Mrs Foster into the kitchen.

David hesitated. Then he ran upstairs, pulled on the hated yellow jacket and hurried out of doors.

It was 8th July. It was the day of the circle. He knew in his guts that it was reaching a climax. He walked down the road, not knowing where to go. He didn't want to be on his own – couldn't call on his father – couldn't very well call on Tim. But there wasn't anybody else.

He turned in the direction of Tim's house, but before he got there he saw the two of them coming towards him down the road.

Jane broke from Tim and ran ahead to David. It was the first time he had seen her act spontaneously. She caught hold of his arm. 'It's now!' she said. Tears poured down her face though she didn't seem to be crying. 'It's now. It's all now and it's terrible. What can we do? Can't we go and see him?'

'We don't know where he is,' said David. 'Anyway it's too late.'

Tim caught up. 'Everything's gone mad,' he said. 'She's gone off her head and our toilet's gone into reverse. Very nasty, I can tell you. We've got to call for the plumber – we can't stop.'

'I'll come with you,' said David. 'Can I come with you?'

'Do what you like.'

The plumber was just putting his phone back on its hook as they went in. Tim explained the problem, briefly but graphically.

'*Your* toilet's gone wrong,' said the plumber. 'Everybody's bloody toilet's gone wrong. And every tap washer in town seems to have perished at exactly the same moment. The lad's out already – there's only one of me – and *my* toilet's gone wrong, too. Does anybody bother to think of *that*?'

The phone began to ring again. The plumber snatched a pencil from behind his ear and broke it in half. 'I can't be everywhere.'

'It's all right,' said David, feeling very, very excited. Then, to Tim and Jane, 'Come on!'

'This is it, isn't it?' said Jane. 'This is it?'

'Yes,' said David.

'It's to do with the flooding,' said Tim.

'This is more than just flooding,' said David. 'Look, look what I've seen. Come out here.'

He pointed to the drain at the side of the road. Dark brown water was bubbling up out of it and the gutter was turning into a small river.

'And over there!' David pointed diagonally across the road. 'Look at that one!'

'Water always comes up drains when there's a flood,' said Tim.

'It's more, much more,' said David. 'Come on. Come and see the circle. It'll be electric now.'

He hustled them both back down the main street where people were beginning to come out of doorways. From what they were saying it appeared that water was coming up every lavatory and down every tap. Nothing would stop it – no one could get hold of a plumber – everyone was asking everyone else what to do.

'Come on,' called David, and he felt as wild and excited as if a moorland wind had got into his soul.

As they passed the chemist shop there was a weird, scattered smashing sound which halted them and drew them inside. It seemed that almost every bottle in the place was broken around the neck, with the liquid streaming out. The pharmacist was standing behind the counter, clasping his hands in front of him.

'Look,' he was saying, almost to himself.

In front of him was a trayful of thermometers. Every one of them had exploded and the liquid mercury rolled and gleamed and bubbled on the tray among the glass fragments.

There were more crashes as more bottles broke where they stood on their shelves.

'Get out,' said the pharmacist urgently. 'You'll be cut. Everybody get out.' He followed them outside.

'Come *on*,' David called. He felt like the Pied Piper leading them through the streets, except that he didn't know why he was leading them – and anyway he wasn't leading them, it was the stones. They were calling to him and they were calling to Jane and they had even caught Tim.

'That's why teeth ache,' said David. 'It's the mercury, the liquid mercury in the fillings being called out. All liquid is being called – that's why Jane's crying. *I'm* crying,' he added in surprise, tasting salt on his own lips. 'But I'm happy.'

He didn't really know if he was happy or not. He wanted to shout, he wanted to sing. His blood raced. He could feel it, actually feel its movement.

And the ground shook very slightly under their feet with the explosion as they passed the pub. Every beer barrel in the cellar had burst, every wine bottle had fired its cork and was pouring forth its offering.

More and more people were in the streets.

'It's the circle,' David was calling aloud, hardly aware that he called it. 'It's the circle, it's the circle.'

He had hold of Jane's hand, now, and Tim was close beside him.

When they reached the bridge, running now, there were other people behind them. Their voices were loud, and their loud voices were almost drowned by the roaring of the river, now up to the level of the bridge. But even that could not drown the thundering of the new waterfall that gushed down the cleft so powerfully that it was clearly visible from the town side of the river. It poured down, throwing spray feet into the air, and it washed across the road and was lost in the brown swirling waters of the river itself.

Never had they ascended the soggy incline so quickly. And when the stones came into sight they glowed, they truly glowed. And the chanting mill could still be heard above the rushing water.

With the greatest of difficulty David held Jane back from touching the stones. 'No, too strong, too strong,' he said.

Tim came up on her other side and caught hold of her arm. He looked across her head at David. 'OK, I believe you,' he said. 'What do we do?'

'The mill,' said David.

'Come on,' said Tim. 'If they won't stop it we'll smash the machinery.'

'You mean it?'

Others had climbed the slope behind them, were sliding in the mud, sinking ankle deep in it, gazing on the glowing stones.

'It's the circle. It *is* the circle,' said David, and Jane took up the chant, seemingly so full of emotion that she hardly knew what to do with herself. She shook her head from side to side. 'It's there and here,' she said. 'Get it out of me.'

'Come back, you're too close,' said David.

Sirens screamed in the town below as firefighters and police struggled to pump out water when there was nowhere to pump it to – to bring order out of the traffic chaos – to let an ambulance through. Overhead, the sound of a police surveillance helicoptor grated across the sky. Even from high on the ridge, they could see the streets were about a metre deep in brown water. People were wading about in it, but no one seemed to know where to direct their efforts.

Closer to, a man strode purposefully up the slope towards the stones, his face grim, an axe ready in his hand.

'No!' said David, his voice hoarse and nearly worn away. 'No! That won't do it!'

But the emergency was too great for anyone to stop and think. Every house in the town was flooded from within and from without. Water poured from taps, ran down walls, swept down stairs. All liquid containers burst their stoppers or shattered. Furniture began to bob in rooms. And the clear water from inside met the dark sewer water outside and whirlpools were created in doorways. And people felt a rising and surging in their own bodies that made hands shake, tears flow and sensations of panic break in waves.

The ring of ancient stones glowed and seemed to hum and the man took his axe to it. The axe struck what seemed like a bolt of lightning out of the tallest stone. The man fell over backwards, the axe head shattered and his arm broken.

The three children began to run and slither down towards the mill, passing others floundering up the slope, including Peter Garrett and the cameraman, and behind them, though not with them, an unexpected figure – Westwood.

'You're back!' said David, hesitating, sliding a little where he stood.

'Out on bail,' said Westwood quietly.

'It's the sound of the mill – working on the stones . . .'

'Was it you? Did you solve it?'

'Yes.'

'You did well. I should have got it – I should have made the connection – but it took a leap of the imagination, and my mind doesn't leap any more . . .'

'Come on!' Tim called, below him.

'I have to go,' said David.

They stumbled on, intent on doing whatever was necessary to stop the machinery. But the mill gave off silence even before they reached it and by the time they were near, everybody was hurrying out, set free to see to the disasters and emergencies that had struck their homes.

The mill, deadline or no deadline, had been closed down.

David took off his jacket and spread it on the mushy ground. Without a word they all sat on it, exhausted beyond measure. They were sitting on a sloping piece of ground, above the mill and not far to the right of the cleft, which they had skirted in their last dash. The waterfall still thundered on.

After a few moments they had to get up because the jacket was sliding them slowly downwards, like a toboggan.

'It's over now,' said David. 'But I don't know how long it'll take to die down.' He looked at Jane. 'How do you feel?'

'Tired.'

'Yes. But – churning?'

'Too tired to know,' said Jane. She stood and considered a moment. 'No. Not churning now. I didn't do it right, did I?'

'How do you mean?'

Jane's hair draggled wetly over her face, just as it had the first time David had set eyes on her, but she looked straight at him and answered directly. 'He said it would be a difficult time for me, and it was, but I meant to be very brave. But now I think about it, I remember screaming and crying.'

'We all were,' said David. 'If you hadn't, you'd probably have exploded – like those bottles.'

She made a face. 'Revolting!'

'Come back to the stones with me,' said David, collecting up an armful of jacket and mud and summoning what energy he had left. 'They need not be damaged.'

'Even now you're not in touch with life,' said Tim.

David stopped in his tracks. 'What?'

No answer.

'*What*? You believed me at last. You were coming to the mill with us.'

119

'Yes,' said Tim. 'You were right. He was right. But now it's all over it doesn't matter if they hammer those old stones to bits to get rid of their anger. What matters now is to go back to the town and start clearing up.'

'Yes,' said David. 'I'm sorry. I will help. But first – they need *not* damage the circle.'

'They mustn't,' said Jane. 'It isn't bad.'

'You come on down,' said Tim. 'We need to help our Mam.'

Jane looked at David.

'It isn't his town,' said Tim. 'Why should he care?'

'You go,' said David to Jane. 'I'll do my best.'

He turned towards the circle and came face to face with his father.

'You stopped the mill,' said Professor Birch.

'No. It stopped anyway.'

David's father turned to look in the direction of the Weeping Stones. 'I apologize for not taking you seriously,' he said. 'Need any help?'

'Yes,' said David. 'Don't let them damage the stone circle.'

'The police are up there – they'll control any vandalism.'

'Yes, but they don't know what really happened – nor do the TV lot - they're up there, too. Tell them what it really was. Tell them all. Explain to them . . .'

'That's your job.'

'I'd rather you did it.'

'You stood on your own before. Can't you now?'

'They won't listen to me,' said David. 'They'll listen

120

to you, and that's all that matters.'

'I'll be with you,' said his father. 'You do the talking – and I'll back you all the way. All right?' He turned and headed up the hillside.

'How's the mosaic?' said David, sliding along in his wake.

'Covered over completely. But we'll clear it again. We'll get whatever co-operation we need now. Westwood'll almost certainly get the first official funding of his life. As of now, this is the most important area in Britain, archaeologically speaking.'

Two days later, when the flood waters had receded, the clearing up was well underway, and the volunteers were beginning to reveal the mosaic once more, David slipped away. He climbed the moorland slope with some hazy idea of bringing comfort to the Weeping Stones, alone and at peace now, their spring almost wholly dried up. He stepped into the centre of the circle, but there could be no communication. He was alone, flesh and blood in a community of stone, an alien community which was somehow conscious in a way he could never understand.

He left the Weeping Stones, standing, leaning, alone on a moorland ridge, and went down the slope to rejoin humanity.

Another Hodder Children's book

THE BURNING

Judy Allen

His image slithered across an old cottage window and again his thin white hands were reflected briefly in the glass, and somewhere inside, in a dark quiet place, the smallest imaginable tremor moved the air. It was not like a full awakening. Not yet. But something that had lain in such deep peace that it might almost not have existed was now a little near the surface than it had been . . .

To Jan and Kate the changes are imperceptible. An attic re-opened after years lying sealed. A stranger seeking answers to family mysteries. A bonfire kindling on a village green that bears the scars of a terrible fire decades ago. But below the surface of their village, something begins its search – for somewhere to feed and grow, for someone to embrace its awesome, slumbering power . . .

THE SPRING ON THE MOUNTAIN

Judy Allen

The murmuring from the new waterfall was a musical sound and it rose and fell like a chant, at once soothing and compelling. He caught himself listening for words in it. He had never been up a mountain in a storm before but he couldn't believe that this darkness, such a short time after noon, could be normal. He was seriously frightened. He looked up into the darkness where the peaceful chanting water was hidden. It was a comforting noise and he was sure it was quite near . . .

On holiday in a cottage at the foot of a Welsh mountain, Emma, Michael and Peter become fascinated by the legends that surround it and by Arthur's Way, the old, straight track that leads to its summit. Then they meet the enigmatic Mrs White and learn of her obsession with the spring on the mountain's top. So is it her strange quest that draws them up Arthur's Way at the most dangerous time of the year? Or is there some ancient power emanating from the spring itself.